FINDERS KEEPERS

THE AGE OF APOPHIS

KAJUAN SMITH

MAURICE MYERS

Eyeconic Entertainment

Email: beeyeconic@eyeconicentertainment.com

Website: www.eyeconicentertainment.com

ISBN:

Printed in the United States of America

First Printing, 12-20-2023

KaJuan's Dedication

To my hive, my core, I love you with everything I have. Without your lessons of love and the purity of your existence, I would've never found the magic in this realm, and this book would have never been born. Mom, Dad, Ke, Kaila, Grandma, and Auntie, thank you!

To Sylvia, there is no combination of words to express what you mean to me. You made me believe I would be a writer and look at me now! I hope you are watching with pride from above.

To Dave, thank you, bro, for sticking by our side every single step of the way. Without you, none of this comes to life. Thank you for being you!

To Kira, the love of my life, my better half, my queen, thank you for being my true north. Thank you for your sacrifice and the space to create something that fulfills my spirit. I love you.

To my sun and moon, my inspirations, I love you. Watching you grow has inspired me to create something I pray you will grow to be proud of. I hope this book inspires you to do whatever your heart desires, for that is what the journey to complete this book has been for me. I love you Kasai and Kahlani.

Maurice's Dedication

To my mama, who always has the answers to all of my problems, thank you. Mama, without you, I wouldn't be able to have the confidence to know I have this type of book in me. Your grace and strength inspire me every day. Thank you for helping me find my purpose.

Padrito, I need to thank you for helping me make this process of becoming a man easier than it was for you. Your growth as a father and a man is always noticed, and I appreciate all that you do for not only me but everyone around you.

Duuges, if anybody knows what it took to get here, it's my baby brother. I hope this book is something that makes you proud and you can always remember me by.

KaJuan and Fleet, our silent assassin, we did this shit! Enough said.

To the countless Friends and Family who have gone on this journey with us, thank you for your opinions, your ear, your PATIENCE, and most of all, your support. It's so many people I would love to thank, but the book is long enough as it is, so if you've been around, this is for you. Thank you, and I hope you enjoy the Finders Keepers Universe.

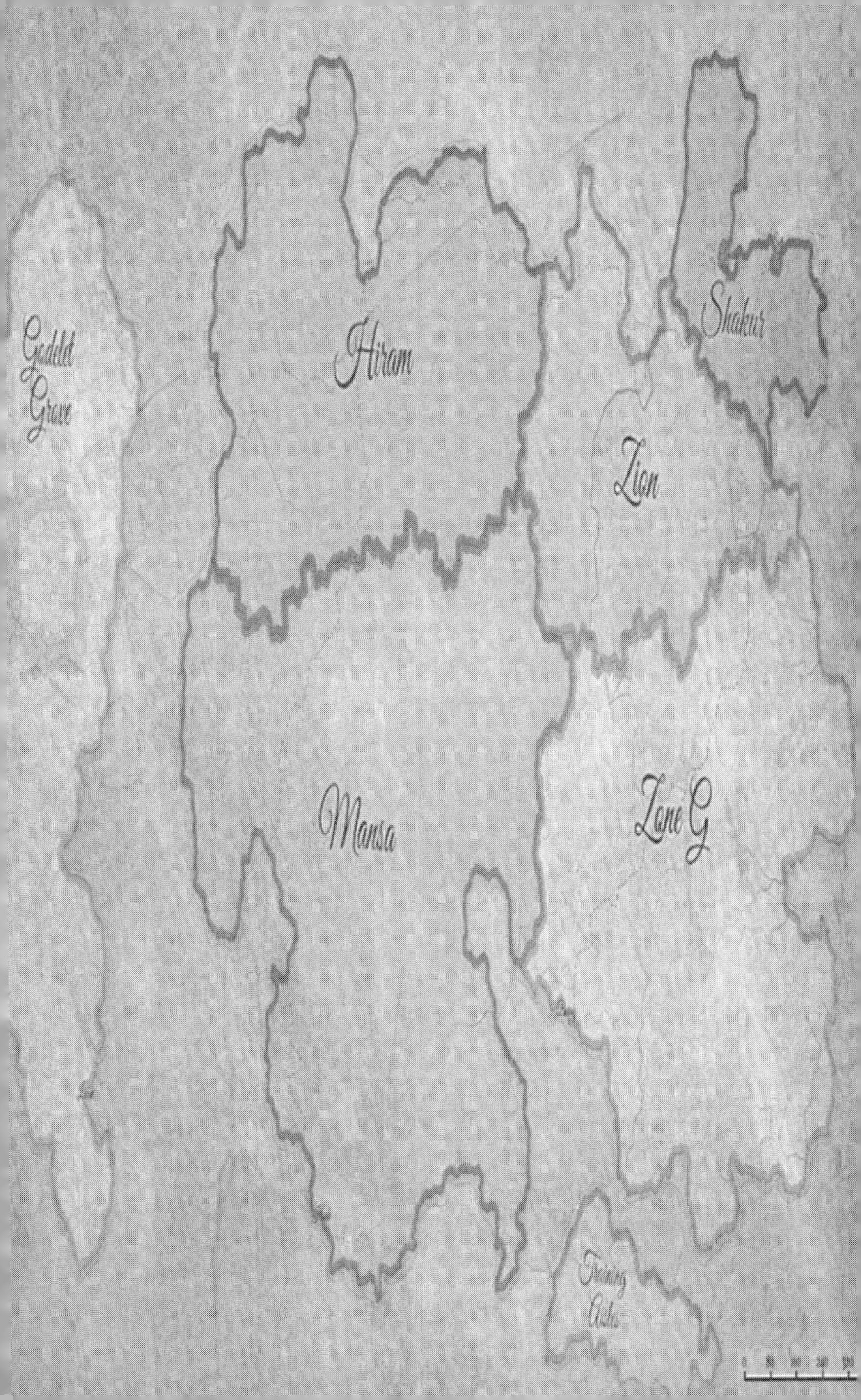
Gaddet Grave
Hiram
Shakur
Zion
Mansa
Zone G
Training

PROLOGUE

B e still," Lando whispered urgently to his comrade.
With a firm grip on Muldrow's bony shoulders, he pulled him down, seeking refuge behind the safety of a nearby wildflower bush. Concealed within the electric blue petals, Lando peered cautiously through the branches, but the impenetrable darkness swallowed everything beyond a few feet. The oppressive heat made it difficult to draw breath and sweat trickled down his brow as he tried to find a way to steady his nerves.

"Do you see them? Can you spot any of the others, Lando?" Muldrow's voice quivered with trepidation.

"Can't see a damn thing out here," Lando grumbled. "Ain't no telling where Remy and the rest of them went."

"Man, we are never going to make it." Muldrow clung to his tattered shirt, his blade tightly gripped, as cold steel pressed against his chest. Fear rendered him trembling; his pants soiled with the weight of fear. He gazed at Lando, a grizzled veteran of countless battles, yearning for his strength and courage. Were it not for him, he surely would have met his demise long ago.

"Pull yourself together! Do you want to be torn apart like the others?" Lando's voice growled low. "Be still!"

A faint hiss began to permeate the air, gradually intensifying until it enveloped them from all sides. The pursuing horrors remained hidden in the cloak of night, yet their chilling hisses echoed, a haunting tone that could only be crafted from nightmares. Even Lando's indomitable courage wavered as the shrill hissing multiplied around them. Suddenly, tiny, malevolent yellow eyes pierced through the darkness, their purity almost seductive. A flock of birds took flight from a nearby tree, causing Muldrow's heart to nearly stop.

"We have to move now!" Lando bellowed, leaping out of the bush and dashing in the opposite direction of the chilling yellow eyes. "Don't look back. Just run, you fool!"

Muldrow struggled to keep pace; his legs spent from the relentless pursuit. The distance between them grew with each passing moment until Lando was devoured by the all-encompassing night. Running blindly, Muldrow knew that slowing down even for an instant would seal his fate. He fought through the agony of exhaustion with every step until the ground vanished beneath him.

Suddenly, Muldrow lost contact with the Earth. It took him by surprise, and he found himself tumbling down an incline, dirt and leaves blurring his vision. He finally came to an abrupt halt as he crashed against the trunk of a gnarled, hollowed Magnolia tree. A sharp pain throbbed in his knee from the fall. He attempted to rise, but his injured leg buckled under his weight.

The bone-chilling hissing grew louder as Muldrow crawled amidst leaves and twigs, desperately seeking some form of shelter from the clutches of death. Panicked, he fought to his feet, hopping on one leg, minimizing the pressure on his injured limb. Struggling to fight through the forest, he dragged his wounded leg behind him until a colossal hand seized him by the back of his collar, yanking him into the hollow trunk of another decaying tree.

His heart fluttered when he saw Lando standing so close that their chests nearly touched, his finger pressed against his lips, urging him to be quiet. The rustling of leaves and crackling of kindling grew nearer, and Muldrow felt the creatures dart past their hollowed sanctuary, a mere flash of leering yellow eyes and shadowy figures. Initially, a few, then a dozen, which quickly multiplied to several dozen, until the forest finally fell into an eerie stillness once more.

Muldrow, paralyzed by fear, looked to Lando for guidance. He watched as Lando cautiously poked his head out from the tree to survey their surroundings. Satisfied that the coast was clear, he emerged from the hollowed-out trunk and assisted Muldrow.

"We still have a long way to go, and your leg isn't looking too promising," Lando whispered. "If we want to survive, we must fight our way out of this."

Muldrow could scarcely find words to respond. He knew he couldn't endure a fight, especially in his current condition. He could feel the swelling slowly encircling his knee, restricting much of his movements.

"Come on now," Lando urged, grabbing Muldrow's arm and draping it around his neck. "We're good as dead if we stay here. Their vision isn't all that great. It looks like they rely on their hearing more than anything. If we stay quiet, we stand a chance."

Lando motioned to proceed, but Muldrow winced in pain, a soft whimper escaping him before Lando promptly hushed him.

"You must be quiet now, or you're going to get us killed," he warned.

"I'm trying. It hurts so bad."

Lando attempted to move once more, to no avail. Switching sides, he tried again, causing Muldrow to flinch and reach for his knee.

"Just leave me behind," Muldrow murmured. "I... I won't make it."

"STOP IT!" Lando's voice growled fiercely. "Do you want to die here?"

Muldrow wiped his eyes and nose, his voice barely audible. "No."

"Then let's go," Lando declared, seizing his arm again.

Muldrow winced but clung on, enduring the pulsating agony. He did his utmost to keep pace with Lando's stride, yet the pain consumed him. Groans and grunts accompanied his every step, but he persisted until the hissing returned.

Once again, they found themselves submerged. It was only a matter of time before the horde of yellow eyes would reappear. Lando struggled, yet his eyes burned with determination and grit, a resolve Muldrow had never witnessed before, especially not directed at him. In his heart, he couldn't let him die on his behalf.

Suddenly, Muldrow withdrew his arms from Lando's grasp.

"Go. I'll fend them off. It's pointless for both of us to die," Muldrow urged.

"We don't have time for this," Lando reached out, but Muldrow staggered away, nearly collapsing.

"No. One of us must return and inform the council of what's unfolding. Trust me, I don't plan on dying here."

After a few moments, Lando shook his head and vanished into the darkness, leaving Muldrow alone in a clearing within the forest. Clutching his dagger tightly, he awaited the inevitable as the hissing multiplied, pervading his senses until it became all he heard. Finally, a pair of yellow eyes emerged from a bush directly ahead, fixating upon him, studying him.

"Come on," Muldrow commanded, summoning every ounce of courage. "Come on, you bastard!"

Emerging from the shadows slithered a beast seemingly crafted from the deepest recesses of the realm's soul. Its body was adorned with dark green scales, and its hands and feet were equipped with eagle-like talons. The creature mustered the courage to stand, reaching Muldrow's waist, and screeched with relentless fury into the night sky, revealing rows of razor-sharp teeth. Hissing chirps followed as more sets of eyes emerged, encircling Muldrow.

Slowly, they advanced, each one indistinguishable from the others, tightening their circle until one lunged. Muldrow evaded the attack, yet the pain shot up his leg, causing him to crumple to the ground, howling in agony.

Another seized the opportunity, preparing to sink its teeth into Muldrow's flesh. But before it could, a massive boot punted the creature, sending it crashing into another and scattering the herd. Lando had returned, cleaving another reptilian creature nearly in two. He grabbed Muldrow, yanking him by the remnants of his shirt, helping him scramble to his feet. Muldrow attempted to follow Lando, but the pain of teeth sinking into his leg overwhelmed him. Howling, he collapsed to the ground. With his blade, he fought back against the creature feasting on his thigh, but he knew this was the end. Strength abandoned him as Lando stood there, watching in horrified silence.

Desperate to assist but overwhelmed, Lando witnessed the creatures swarm, choosing to devour the defenseless prey.

"GO... SURVIVE!" Those were the last words Lando heard from Muldrow as the reptilian creatures showed no mercy, tearing his body to pieces. Lando sprinted with all his might, cutting through trees and slashing at the remaining reptilians in pursuit. He ran until there was nowhere left to flee—a cliff's edge stood before him. Below stretched fields of oozing yellow eggs, pods filled with more maturing reptilians for as far as the eye could see.

"Oh... my... God," Lando stammered, gazing out over the grotesque expanse. "This... can't be."

In an instant, a sharp, piercing pain struck his chest. Breathing became laborious as he looked down to see what appeared to be a spear emerging from his torso. Only then, as he felt himself lifted into the air, did he realize it was the tail of a creature much larger than the ones that had pursued him. This creature, marked with black patterns across its muscular form, towered over him, locking eyes with him.

With a swift flick of its tail, the larger reptilian creature hurled Lando to the ground. Helpless, he watched as the creature loomed above him, hissing into the night sky. Lowering its scaled face, it exhaled a warm, putrid breath that caressed Lando's cheek, examining him intently. It licked him several times with its long, forked tongue, and a warm sensation washed over him. Within seconds, he lost control, unable to move any part of his body. Then, slowly, yellow eyes emerged one by one, encircling him.

Lando inhaled deeply, his senses tingling as familiar cries pierced through the eerie hiss of the forest. Emerging from the dense woods, a sinuous reptilian figure dragged a wild woman, her defiant cries echoing until a ruthless backhand silenced her, forcing her to her knees.

With a swift, graceful bow, the reptilian retreated into the shadowy woods, leaving the wild woman standing there, her presence as stark as a sacrificial offering. The larger reptilian, a sinister figure, circled her like an evil phantom, its tail sharp as a spear and still dripping with Lando's blood, flicking through the air as it whispered ominously.

"You are now mine," it hissed, words dripping with malevolence. "You will bear witness to your friend's demise, a reminder of what happens when you try to escape."

Seizing the woman by the nape of her neck forced her to stand upright. At that moment, she finally recognized Lando lying helplessly on the forest floor.

"Remy," Lando's voice echoed through the tension, desperation lacing his words.

"I'm here!" she cried out, her trembling hand brushing her mouth, her gaze locked helplessly onto Lando's strained smile.

"Survive," he implored, a heartfelt plea concealed within those whispered words.

With a sinister hiss, the smaller reptilians closed in, their predatory instincts taking control, encircling him with relentless hunger, to Remy's horror, until all that remained was an eerie stillness and the haunting emptiness of the forest.

CHAPTER I
IN THE BEGINNING
CAIRO

After I rank number one, the whole realm will agree that I deserve to be king!" Cairo's voice reverberated through the air as his holographic surfboard, adorned in shades of green, tore through the pristine waves of the ocean. The sun's warm caress against Cairo's rich, warm caramel, brown-colored skin sent waves of pleasure coursing through his body, while his tightly naturally coiled high-top fade absorbed the water, growing heavier with each passing moment.

Attached to the back of his surfboard was a hover cart carrying his younger brother, who clung to the sides, eyes lit with excitement. Little Ja'el, his afro, bobbed and weaved in rhythm with the rolling waves, his almond-colored small hands gripping the cart tightly, desperate to avoid being thrown headfirst into the unforgiving waves.

Using his heel, Cairo pressed a mechanism near the rear of his board, unleashing a surge of speed as he ascended a towering wave capable of swallowing buildings whole. At the wave's zenith, his gaze fell upon a girl with warm amber, brown-colored skin and a flowing cascade of natural curls tinted a mesmerizing shade of blue.

Unfortunately, her presence was a momentary distraction, causing Cairo to mistime his launch, resulting in the full force of the waves crashing upon him and his brother, burying them deep into the watery abyss.

Cairo skillfully maneuvered through the water like a creature born of the sea, rescuing his brother by the hand and guiding him back to the surface. Concern etched his face, "Are you alright, Ja'el?" He examined his baby brother, hoping for no signs of harm.

Ja'el, still breathless from unintentionally inhaling seawater, managed to nod and flash a thumbs-up, indicating his well-being. A sigh of relief escaped Cairo's lips as he cradled Ja'el on his back, making their way toward the shore. He leisurely swam back to the ivory sands, fueled by a profound sense of embarrassment. Thus, he felt a surge of relief upon realizing the princess of Zone G had not witnessed the incident; her back turned to the spectacle.

Upon reaching the shore, Cairo inspected his brother again, his heart dreading the sound of his mother's anger over any harm that might have occurred to the youngest member of their family. "Are you sure you're okay?" he asked again, his eyes searching Ja'el's face.

A sparkle of youthful enthusiasm ignited within Ja'el as he responded with an energetic smile, "Yeah, I'm good! That was pretty scary, but I knew you would save me. Let's do it again!"

"Aww, Cairo, is everyone alright?" a concerned voice called out from a distance.

Standing on the boardwalk adjacent to the beach were three teenage boys engaged in snickering banter. The fair-skinned Maaku, garbed in preppy attire, took the lead in the mocking while his badger-rat-faced lackeys, Iggy and Ian, reveled in their roles like the followers they were.

Cairo offered a sarcastic smile, doing his best to ignore their presence as he passed by, but Maaku persisted in hurling insults and taunting him about his wipeout. As they walked on, Cairo couldn't help but notice Ja'el clenching his tiny fists tightly at his sides.

"Look, guys, the useless prince of Mansa can't even handle a little water, *and this guy* thinks he's going to overstep his brother and become king someday," Maaku sneered, inciting an eruption of laughter from his lackeys.

"SHUT UP!" Ja'el erupted, his voice charged with a determination far beyond his years.

Ja'el lunged forward, intent on confronting them, but Cairo swiftly scooped him up, diffusing the situation. Maaku, Ian, and Iggy cackled with amusement, pointing and mimicking the toddler prince.

"Maaku, quit playing with me," Cairo stated, clutching Ja'el tightly under his arm, fighting against his brother's persistence.

"Ian and Iggy, remember that face. It's the same face he'll make when they announce my name as the number one ranked cadet tonight," Maaku retorted, his words oozing with arrogance.

"Everyone saw on that training island what I'm about, so we'll let the judges have the final say today," Cairo shot back.

"You better turn on Second Thought and listen to what everybody is saying on TV. Neither you nor Kane stand a chance in the rankings. The entire island will see just how second-rate the King's sons truly are tonight," Maaku declared.

Ian and Iggy erupted in another round of laughter as if on cue, desperately attempting to stroke their boss's ego. However, the atmosphere shifted when Ja'el wriggled free from Cairo's grasp and kicked Iggy in the leg. Iggy made a motion, ready to retaliate against the young prince, but Cairo swiftly removed his ring, transforming it into a customized staff. Cairo spun his staff, creating a barrier between Ja'el and Iggy. In one quick motion, Cairo struck Iggy's heels with the staff, toppling him to the ground with a resounding thud that shook the boardwalk.

A swift swing followed, the metal tip of the staff connecting with Iggy's mouth as the blade released from his staff, transforming into a scythe. Cairo restrained him, preventing him from getting up as the blade sat up against Iggy's neck, casting a defiant gaze at Ian and Maaku, silently urging them to intervene. Ian ran over, and Cairo lifted his scythe and held him at bay. Maaku, however, stood rooted in place.

Instead, he motioned for Cairo to look behind him. To his horror, Cairo discovered a gathering crowd, capturing the exchange through their lenses. Cairo deftly retracted his scythe into his sleek, enchanted ring and wordlessly grasped Ja'el's arm. Negative portrayals of him splattered across various media platforms were the last thing he needed on the day he aspired to claim the title of highest-ranking cadet in the latest training cohort.

Just as he prepared to navigate through the maelstrom of media, a towering figure clothed in a well-tailored suit, his complexion, a rich brown hue, abruptly appeared in front of Cairo. The crowd instinctively yielded; their clamoring cameras silenced. Cairo instinctively mimicked the man's actions, attempting to shield both his and his brother's faces from the prying eyes of onlookers. Once they managed to break free from the mayhem, the man turned to them, flashing a nervous smile.

"Greetings... uh, well, I am Manny. It is my honor to serve as your support under the guidance of your mother. She uh...she sent me to retrieve the two of you. She wants you both to understand that she is NOT happy."

"Manny, right? Well, it's nice to meet you, and thank you for all that back there. But I had to do what I had to do, you know?" Cairo replied, his words a blend of courtesy and firm resolve.

"I get it, sir. I understand. Let's get you out of here."

Manny quickly summoned a hover car to transport them back to the confines of their palace. Much to Cairo's delight, the journey proved much longer than usual. The streets teemed with congestion as the city bustled with preparations to welcome the inhabitants of the remaining three villages for the grandest celebration of the year.

As they arrived at the palace, Cairo and Ja'el were sure to slip through the grand entrance, as quiet as a housecat, eager to evade their mother's scolding. Fortune smiled at them as she was nowhere to be found, prompting them to run to Cairo's room. Time was of the essence as he hastened to freshen up and change before his big day. Meanwhile, Ja'el hopped onto Cairo's aquamarine bed, channel surfing for any festival coverage.

A familiar face captured Cairo's attention. Stephen B, renowned for his passionate, unfiltered tirades, defended his chosen cadets, reverberating through the airwaves.

"What you are failing to realize here is that this is the largest class we've ever had in the realm's history, alright! So, being considered for top five honors out of one hundred cadets would mean you've got to be special!

We already know you have the brothers Kane and Cairo Amaan, the sons of the great King Alo and Queen Nebi, who have enormous pressure on their shoulders. Prince Vadé of Hiram, I'm hearing is up there, Princess Mariella of Zone G and her friend Serenity did great, and even the newly appointed Prince Donovan of Zion showed out we get all of that, BUT from what I hear, it's the princes of Mansa that have felt that pressure and responded. With all that said, I still don't know if either of them did enough to knock Maaku out of that top-ranked spot, though."

"Give me your top five right now, Steven B," the gorgeous moderator asked.

"You know what? I'll give it later in the show. Before we go off the air, I'll drop my top five."

"I'll tell you right now, if Maaku is outside of your top three, you need to be drug tested, Steven B," the second analyst said, "That kid is absolut —"

Frustrated, Cairo quickly switched off the television, tossing the remote aside.

They better not rank him number one, Cairo seethed silently, squinting at the screen, consumed by the prospect of Maaku gloating over outranking him.

"Don't worry, Cairo, you'll be number one, and if not, then Kane will get it."

"Hopefully, you're right, Ja. Now head out and get ready before mommy realizes I had you on the beach today, and Kane becomes an only child."

A knock resounded on the door, interrupting their conversation.

"Come in," Cairo called.

"Yoo cuzzos!!" came a shrill voice from behind the door.

Stepping inside was Vadé, a tall and slender copper-skinned teenager in a stunning blue suit adorned with subtle gold accents. The square emblem on his blazer proudly displayed a golden H, representing Hiram, his hometown. A diamond-encrusted golden watch decorated his wrist, complementing his square-framed glasses.

"What's up lil man, you ready for today?"

"I'm ready for everything, ah," Ja'el yelled as he hit Vade and ran past him.

Ja'el sped off down the hallway to his room, and Vadé swiftly closed the door behind them, "Where's Kane?"

"I don't know. I think he's at Ganyah's. What's up?"

"Yo, what the hell happened on the beach today? Why are you out here beating people up? You can't just wait til the quest for all that." Vade joked.

"Man, they started with me, but I'm not trying to talk about that right now; I'm trying to focus on rankings."

"Well, you're the only one not trying to talk about it; it's everywhere. Stephen B is even setting up a segment about it later."

"Alright, Vadé, damn!"

"My fault; let me move on before you get mad and start hitting people again. I wanted to talk to you about something important anyway. There's a lot going on out here. Did Auntie mention anything to you?"

"Nah, I've been avoiding Mom since we returned from the beach. What's up?"

"I heard my parents talking about how the King and Queen of Zion have been moving funny lately. My mother was pissed."

"Funny how?"

"She kept ranting about how they've been a thorn in the council's side since they took the throne. I think they're talking about gaining independence from the rest of the villages."

"Independence?" Cairo queried; his face contorted in confusion.

"Exactly," Vadé confirmed, clapping his hands for emphasis. "Kane kept saying something wasn't right since we got back from training."

"To hell with them; we just spent a year training; tonight is the festival. I'm not letting them mess up my day." Cairo dismissed with a wave of his hand.

"Nah, you don't understand; the council discussed possibly postponing the festival. Something about things has been short."

Cairo's heart plummeted, sinking to the floor. "Why in the hell would they do that for? Is it that bad?"

"I don't know. The phone rang while my parents were talking and messed everything up. But listen," Vadé leaned in, "I know Shareeva has been spending a great deal of time in Zion lately. This can't be a coincidence that now Zion suddenly turns shady."

"Shareeva? See, man, that's your aunt."

"That's your aunt too, don't try that. She barely acknowledges I exist," said Vadé. "I hope she's not part of anything foul this time around."

"She's always doing something," Cairo seethed, his nostrils flaring angrily. "Ain't she supposed to be staying in Shakur anyway?"

"She probably is up to something, but then again, I feel like I could be being paranoid. She really does stay out the way these days."

"I don't put anything past her. She was in love with the most notorious enemy in Umoyan history!"

"Her and Shakur happened thousands of years ago, Cairo; you know she can't go back to the dark side after she turned on him."

"I guess," Cairo replied, his voice filled with dissatisfaction. "I put up with her out of respect for Mom, but she's the same person who turned on her people from where I'm standing."

"You sound just like Mars. He was on the same type of time when I spoke with him earlier. Did you know he left the palace in Zone G?"

"Did he leave, or was he kicked out? Mariella told me last night that their parents kicked him out again because he was on that stuff. Now he's out here in that RV selling food."

"Yeah, well, Mars do be on that stuff, so when they accused him of hallucinating, I kind of couldn't be mad at them," Vadé added.

"Hallucinating?" Cairo asked, shaking his head in disbelief.

"Yeah, man, he mentioned Auntie Reevie in the woods and even said he saw an Igandhi. We couldn't get into it too much 'cause we were in public, and you know how he gets."

"Igandhi? The reptilians?" Cairo said, shaking his head, "Damn, he must be over there high off of his supply."

"That whole family is nuts, but you're the one trying to marry into it."

"I'm bringing Mariella into my kingdom, good brother. That nonsense they get away with over in Zone G will have to stay over there, but that's a conversation for when I become king."

"When you become King, huh? It's hard to believe you're still stuck on that, "Vadé chuckled sarcastically. "Between that and a dragon, you sure got some big dreams, huh?"

Cairo felt a pinch of offense at Vadé's audacity, but over the years, he had grown accustomed to his cousin's comments and brushed them off.

"You don't know what you are talking about because when it's all said and done, I will have a dragon and be king."

"Cairo, I'm not even addressing the dragon comment. They don't even exist anymore, but it is Kane's right as the eldest to ascend the throne. What makes you think you can defy thousands of years of tradition?"

"My brother told me I could! Both you and I know Kane has no desire to be King. If he doesn't want the throne, then why not me?"

"What happens if the rest of the royal court makes a fuss and does everything in their power to stop you?" Vadé questioned.

"See you not doing the math, cuz. You will run Hiram one day. Mariella is positioned to take charge in Zone G, especially with this Mars situation going on. I will run Mansa in my brother's place, and I'm sure Serenity will find a way to become the Queen. If not, then I will at least have the support of most of the council," Cairo said with a smile, raising an eyebrow. "So, who exactly do you expect to stop us?"

Vadé nodded, partly impressed by Cairo's reasoning. "Touché, cousin. Touché."

"Let's head out and do a few interviews before we hit the streets."

"I'm right with you, cuz," Vadé responded.

Cairo and Vadé made their way down the hallway and descended the stairs before they entered the living room where his aunts awaited them.

"Aw, the two of you look just like your fathers. I can't take it," Aunt Shunny gushed, beaming from ear to ear. "Speaking of your father, Vadé, go outside and see what Safan needs help with before you head downtown."

"Yes, ma'am," Vadé replied, heading out the door.

Shunny turned to Cairo and glided over to her nephew with her long, gorgeous, jet-black curly hair bouncing as she approached.

"How's my favorite aunty doing on this glorious day?" Cairo asked, letting her go.

"I'm as good as can be, my spirit is excited to see you boys up there on stage tonight."

Cairo greeted his other aunt, Shareeva, who offered a rushed and half-hearted hug. Her dry black hair always appeared untamed; her curls so wild they were beginning to lock. She observed her nephew, unimpressed, and with a mere wave of her hand, Cairo's blazer began to adjust itself in a wave of small purple energy.

"Now you look presentable. I don't understand why you boys insist on looking a mess on a day you insist on taking so seriously," Shareeva scowled.

"Today *is* an important day, and you know my father doesn't like you using Apophis's magic in his house," Cairo said, glancing around nervously.

"We've entered the age of Apophis. I figured you were enjoying the shift in energy around here after I saw you out there on that boardwalk," Shareeva teased.

Shunny said from the side, "I'm sure you had your reasons for doing what you did."

"His reason is because it's the Dawn of Apophis, and he feels it in his core. Ain't that right, nephew?" Shareeva sarcastically hurled at Cairo.

"Enough, Reevie," Shunny said, rolling her eyes at Shareeva as she averted her eyes to Cairo. "Are you ready for the big reveal at the festival?"

"I just hope there actually *is* a festival today," Cairo responded flatly.

"What are you talking about?" Shareeva questioned.

"Word on the streets is that the festival might be postponed or something," Cairo explained.

"Who said that?!" Shunny's voice rose with astonishment.

Vadé entered the room, catching a glimpse of his mother's piercing gaze. Cairo looked towards his cousin, who shot him a dirty look from the corner of the living room.

"I'm just telling you what I'm hearing out there. But those are just rumors, right Aunty," Cairo asked, seeking reassurance.

"I want to know who told you something like that," Shunny demanded, her gaze fixed on Vadé.

"They're all just rumors," Nebi's voice said as she entered the kitchen, adjusting her dress.

She looked stunning, dressed in a breathtaking red gown adorned with black diamond accents that sparkled in the light like stars against the night sky. Atop her head rested a crown she had explicitly crafted for the festival.

"Now, normally, I'd be all over you about your little scuffle on the boardwalk earlier, but we have more important things to focus on." Nebi continued and turned to her sisters. "We must head to the stadium and conduct a walk-through before meeting with the council. We have only a few hours, and you know how chaotic the city's traffic will be."

"Yes, boss," said Shareeva, shooting out of her chair and grabbing a handful of bags before heading towards the door.

Nebi shook her head, ignoring Shareeva's sarcasm, and turned to Cairo.

"Now listen," she shifted to a more serious tone, "I better not see any more videos of you attacking anyone else! One more, and it's me and you, do you understand?"

"You know Maaku stay messing with me; I can't just let them punk me, ma."

"Then you need to handle it out of the camera's eye," Nebi said as she caressed Cairo's cheek right before sending her palm across the back of his head and hugging him. "I'm so proud of you," she whispered in his ear. "Now you and your big-headed cousin, get out of here and stay out of trouble," she playfully remarked, patting the back of his head, "I love you."

"I love you too, ma," Cairo responded as he and his cousin stepped out the door, embarking on their journey to the city.

CHAPTER 2
BEHIND THE CURTAIN
KANE

The silence of the fields just beyond the village of Mansa gave Kane a rare solace, one he had seldom known since his return from the training isles. Perched high upon the forest hills overlooking the city, Kane would often find himself seated amidst a sea of grass.

Most Umoyans would not dare to venture so far from the well-trodden paths of merchants and traders. On his quest to escape the clamor of the media and the burdens that accompanied his impending ascension to the Umoyan throne, he discovered a field decorated with tender blades of grass and Lionmouth lilies on the outskirts of the forest.

During the years-long training period on the Umoyan coast islands, he yearned for his secluded haven. Kane found himself captivated by the breathtaking panorama that unfolded before him.

As Kane closed his eyes and inhaled deeply, relishing the warm caress of the sun on his mahogany skin and the gentle whispers of the calming breeze through the forest, a soft voice foreign to him reached his ears, whispering. The multitude of voices was jumbled, making it impossible to decipher a message. Quickly, his eyes opened, scanning the surroundings in search of its source, only to find himself alone. Just as he began dismissing the incident as a figment of his imagination, the voices called out again.

He stood motionless, twirling in circles, determined to resist succumbing to paranoia, but his struggle was quickly defeated. His heart quickened its tempo, thumping hard within his chest as he fruitlessly sought the source of those whispers amidst the forest's tranquility. Suddenly, a rustle in the nearby bushes startled Kane, nearly throwing him into a frenzy, until his beloved father emerged from the woods.

"Dad?"

"It has been a long time since I last visited this place," Alo said, gasping for breath, "I had forgotten how high up it is."

Kane's nerves tingled with curiosity as he nervously scratched the back of his head. "How... How did you find me?"

"Do you think you are the only one looking for a little peace away from all the crazy? This spot might have the best view in the entire realm," Alo remarked, his eyes fixated on the horizon before them.

Kane lowered his head, his laughter echoing within, before feeling the tight embrace of his father's arm encircling his shoulders.

"I just needed a few minutes, Dad," Kane confessed. Alo turned his deep brown eyes toward his son, penetrating Kane's soul.

Alo clicked his tongue, a half-smile gracing his lips. "I know that feeling all too well. You truly are my son," he declared, affectionately ruffling Kane's hair before playfully nudging him away.

"Listen, I know you have a lot of pressure on your shoulders as heir to the Umoyan throne. But I truly believe that you will surpass me one day. I have no doubt that you will grow to be the kind of king the realm needs."

"Thank you, Dad," Kane responded half-heartedly, his voice tinged with a hint of shallowness.

Alo chuckled silently to himself, "You tried your best to mean those words, didn't you?" Alo observed, sporting a half-smile. "Hear me out, son," he continued, kneeling beside Kane, "I know you want to be a Nomad, and there is profound honor in that path. Searching the stars to find our lost brothers and sisters amongst the galaxies has always occupied a special place in my heart. I was even involved in launching that initiative. However..."

"My place is on the throne, I understand, Dad."

Alo drew closer, his brown eyes simultaneously stern and vulnerable, peering into Kane's essence. "When I was your age, I thought about becoming a Nomad with Ganyah, but the Gods had other plans. It took me a long time before I learned that my duty transcended personal desires—to safeguard our future. I urge you to listen to the Gods. Follow them in all things."

As much as he wanted to respond, words failed Kane. His mind whirled, frantically attempting to formulate a response that would avoid sounding utterly foolish. Suddenly, he felt his father's hand beneath his chin, gently lifting his face.

"Come, my son. Tell me what's wrong," Alo implored.

"It's just... At times, I fear I'm losing my grip on reality," Kane admitted, his voice fading like a distant echo on the wind. "I have these dreams, and when I'm alone sometimes..."

A surge of excitement coursed through Alo's eyes, swiftly concealed but not escaping Kane's notice.

"Sometimes what?" Alo asked.

"Sometimes....I hear...voices," Kane said, forcing the words from his lips.

"In my heart, I knew. Listen to their voices," Alo declared firmly. "You are the final child born in the age of the red sun. The spirit of Shango and Yemaya flows deep within our family veins—the only pure-blooded Umoyans to unite their tribes. You, my eldest son, are destined for the throne, not solely by blood but through your profound connection with the Gods. I want you to know that you can always talk to me when it comes to our little unique ability. Many will never know the burdens of the gift, but I do."

Alo's grip tightened upon Kane's shoulder, yet he refrained from flinching. Instead, he mustered a feeble grin in response to his father's words. Revealing his ability to hear the callings was something he could never bring himself to share with anyone, not even his brother Cairo. His father's acceptance offered a much-needed relief from the burden he harbored.

"I understand, Dad."

"Remember, my son, you are not alone in this journey. Your ancestors and the Gods themselves guide you. Embrace your connection with the voices and dreams. Let them be your compass. You have always had a unique spirit, Kane. Trust in yourself and in the path that unfolds before you."

Kane took a deep breath, absorbing his father's words of wisdom. The weight of his destiny now felt more like a shared burden rather than an overwhelming pressure. He now felt a newfound resolve surging within him. In his spirit, he knew he needed to heed his father's advice, embrace his connection with the voices, and navigate the path ahead. His dreams held secrets, and it was time for him to listen to the echoes of the Gods and uncover their meanings.

"Thank you, Dad," Kane said, his voice filled with gratitude and determination. "That really helps pop. I needed that."

"Good. Now, enough hiding in the forest. You need to make your way to Ganyah's house. I've bought your clothes so that you can change there. To the north, there should still be a path near the Blue Widow's patch that will lead you straight to his backyard. No one will see you coming, except Ganyah, of course, because...well, because he's him."

"Thank you, Dad...for everything. I'll see you at the festival." Kane replied.

Don't be late messing around with your brother. It will be too many eyes, and you know your mother wants everything perfect for today. She worked hard with limited resources to put this together. She has a lot in store. This year will definitely be the greatest festival the realm has ever seen!"

"For sure," Kane said.

He embraced his father, feeling the weight of the world lift from his shoulders for the first time in what seemed like an eternity. Once his father disappeared into the thick of the forest, he darted towards Ganyah's. Passing through the entangled hickory trees and the dense canopy of coca oaks, he eventually arrived at the clearing behind his mentor's house. From his vantage point, he could already discern the dwelling bustling with jubilant Umoyans, filling their cups with oils and donning their finest traditional attire.

Kane couldn't help but roll his eyes, his impatience growing as he braced himself for the onslaught of drunken inquiries from the various trainers. He hoped his brother and friends were already present to absorb some of the attention away from himself.

He surveyed the yard, seeking a less crowded spot amongst the inebriated Umoyans. With most guests gathered near the house, he figured he could sneak along the perimeter of Ganyah's property unnoticed. He leaped onto the ten-foot gate behind the alignment of pine trees, landing gracefully on its trimming. Quietly, he tiptoed along until he reached the alleyway between the neighboring yards. He noticed Ganyah's guest bedroom window open three floors above him.

Bracing himself, he climbed up the tree and, using one of the branches, propelled himself upwards to grasp the stone windowsill. With his eyes just above the ledge, he carefully scanned the room to ensure it was empty before silently making his way inside. Half impressed by his stealth, he cracked a half-smile and gently closed the window.

"Good to see you made it," a voice greeted him from behind.

Kane smiled to himself, immediately recognizing his trainer's voice. "How did you know I was here?" Kane groaned, "I know I didn't make a sound."

Ganyah leaned against the door frame, folding his arms. Shaking his head, he regarded his protege. Dressed in his festival attire—a sleek black suit with a black undershirt and matching shoes—Ganyah's signature long, silky black hair neatly tied in a ponytail.

"You're the only Umoyan I know who would rather scale a

building than engage in conversation. Really?" Ganyah remarked, embracing Kane.

"The difficulty level felt about the same, to be honest," Kane quipped.

"Smart ass," Ganyah replied, chuckling. "You can't avoid everyone, especially on a day like today. So go ahead and get changed; meet me downstairs, please. Your brother will be here soon."

"I got you."

"Stay sharp. Your brother made the news earlier today with his little stunt at the boardwalk. So just go out there, be cordial, and get through the day. Any additional attention is something you don't want, right?"

"Yeah, but wait, go back. What happened with Cairo?"

"Turn on the TV, and don't make me come back here to get you," Ganyah said before closing the door behind him.

"Ok, ok," Kane whispered.

He gestured with his hand, igniting the massive television nearly covering the entire wall. The live broadcast of Second Thought filled the screen with a headline at the bottom: "TROUBLE IN PARADISE?" As the screen transitioned to Steven B. delivering a passionate speech, Kane didn't unmute the television, electing to watch his brother's fight. The media cleverly branded the altercation the "Brawl at the Beach."

Kane suddenly shook his head when he saw his face splatter across the screen as the headline at the bottom switched to Steven B's top five predictions.

The only opinion that matters is the festival judges, he thought to himself. He finished dressing in his custom black suit, accented with red diamond-studded loafers and took one last look in the mirror. Switching off the television, he approached the window to gauge the swelling crowd's size before going downstairs.

The crowd had doubled since his discreet escapade. Only after he turned off the television did he hear muffled drunken laughter and the sound of traditional festival music emanating from downstairs.

The foreign voices whispered as he reached for the door to join the festivities.

He spun around in a panic, recalling his father's words in the woods. Do not be afraid. Listen to them.

The mysterious voices continued once more.

Outside the window, Kane noticed something peculiar—falling from the sky, not snowflakes but ash. He approached the window cautiously, realizing nobody below seemed to notice. They continued galivanting about, oblivious to the peculiar spectacle. Rubbing his eyes in disbelief, he hoped it would vanish, but it persisted, falling like wintry flakes. Pressing his face against the glass, he couldn't believe what he was witnessing.

"Kane, what are you doing up here?" Ganyah's disapproving voice broke through.

"Uh, nothing. I was just about to come downstairs," Kane replied, turning back towards the window.

Everything appeared normal—the ash had ceased falling, leaving no trace. Yet, a sense of unease gnawed at Kane's stomach. *Could this be a sign from the gods? What could it possibly mean?* He thought to himself.

"Come on, Kane. Stop playing up here and go greet the rest of the guardians," Ganyah urged.

Kane glanced out the window, reassuring himself that all was well. He followed Ganyah through the halls and down the stairs, where dozens of Umoyans filled the living room. Guardians, cadets, and their loved ones mingled, and a few nervous cadets conversed.

"Well, if it isn't the life of the party."

"Oh hey, what's up, General," Kane said, giving the towering man a fist bump.

He was almost taken aback to see the General dressed in formal attire. His usual wild, bushel of hair and belly-grazing beard were somewhat groomed, partially concealing his round face. In his younger days, Kane believed the General kept his hair unruly to cover his eye patch, but that was before he learned that the General regarded his patch as a championship trophy.

"You havin' fun?" the General boomed, spewing specks of spit everywhere.

"I hope he's having fun. It's his festival day. Ganyah interjected, suddenly appearing behind the General.

Standing beside him was an older man, overwhelmed by the drunken Umoyans staggering around. He extended his wrinkled hand to Kane, offering a feeble smile.

"Nice to finally meet you face to face, Prince Kane. Ganyah always talks about you and your brother, but I haven't had the pleasure. My name is Cephas."

"Well, it's a pleasure to meet you, Cephas."

However, Kane's words were ignored. Cephas was too preoccupied, glancing uncomfortably over his shoulder at anyone who ventured too close.

"Are... are you alright, Mr. Cephas?"

"Could we go outside? I don't want any of these drunken fools to bump into me. I'm not as sturdy as I used to be."

"Sure," Ganyah replied, offering his arm.

Kane and the General led the way, creating a path for Ganyah to guide the elder towards the outdoor deck. Once seated on the oak bench overlooking the sprawling yard, Cephas visibly relaxed. Kane felt grateful for the presence of the older man, as he too longed to escape the intoxicated individuals exchanging drunken war stories.

"I apologize, young man. Too many Umoyans make me nervous?" said Cephas with a twisted smile.

"No need to apologize. Trust me, I get it." Kane replied. "How do you know Ganyah?"

"Oh, ha-ha. Well, I'm the one who taught him everything he knows."

Kane looked at Ganyah, who flashed a sense of embarrassment for the first time in his recollection.

"Alright, old man," Ganyah interjected. "Because you don't know when to stop once you start."

"Come here, child, let me get a good look at you," Cephas beckoned.

Kane shuffled nervously to the older man as he observed him head to toe, "Don't look so nervous. It's alright."

"Cephas has the sight," said Ganyah cryptically, "That's why he doesn't like a bunch of crowds."

Kane watched nervously as Cephas circled him before stopping and looking him in the eyes.

"You were right, Ganyah; he's just like his father. He can hear the callings, too, but this one is running from it. It's like he's waiting for something. Do you mind?" he asked, holding up his hand.

Despite his better judgment, Kane nodded and allowed Cephas to press his thumb firmly against his forehead. Immediately, Kane felt an overwhelming sense of warmth wash over his body as Cephas shut his eyes tight as if deep in concentration. Then his face went blank before he opened his eyes, snatching his hand away as if he was suddenly startled and staring at Kane with a deep sense of wonder.

"The day you stop running from who you are will be the day you unleash a great power that will rival even your fathers."

"Alright already, don't freak the kid out before the festival now," Ganyah cautioned.

"You're right," Cephas said, "Sorry about that."

"It's fine. I was just talking to my father about the same thing."

"Listen to them and trust your gut," Cephas said with a wink.

"Alright, can I trust you to keep an eye on Kane while I get Serenity and Mariella to Shunny's lounge on the southside? I would ask Ark here, but as you can see, he has already had a few too many."

"I'm perfectly fine. What are ya talkin' about?" barked the General, as Cephas chuckled to himself.

"And I do not need a babysitter," Kane interjected.

"Behave yourself," Ganyah commanded sternly before returning to the house.

"Don't worry, young Prince," Cephas smiled. "In all honesty, I am the one who probably needs a babysitter. Old age can be quite overwhelming."

"It's all good. The opposite of growing old is...well, you know. And that option sucks," Kane replied, much to Cephas's delight.

"Do me a favor, would you? Could you fetch me a slice of that delightful wildberry pie they have inside? Of course, I shouldn't be eating it, but what the hell? It's a festival," Cephas shrugged.

"I got you."

Kane rose from the table and navigated through the conversations in the kitchen area, avoiding as many as possible. As he neared the rear doors, specks of ash began descending outside the window. Once again, Kane froze in his tracks. Astonishingly, no one noticed the clear, sunny skies transforming into dense gray clouds, showering the city with ash. Slowly pushing open the doors, he found himself alone. Everyone had vanished, and the backyard lay in ruins.

Not only was the house empty, but destruction enveloped everything he saw. He turned around to behold a once-festive gathering reduced to a near-demolished foundation. The roof had disappeared entirely. Fires ravaged the city, and wreckage, smoke, and ash stretched as far as his eyes could see.

What in the hell is happening? He thought to himself.

Still clutching the pie, he stepped off what remained of the balcony into the yard, littered with craters.

"Kane," a voice called from behind.

Standing on the balcony was an unrecognizable Umoyan man, but as he limped a few steps closer, Kane realized that the Umoyan man was wearing a silver mask. When he got closer, the mysterious man cackled a robotic laugh before ripping his mask off, revealing the prince of Zion Donovan. Yet, he appeared transformed—half-dead, with greenish scales patched throughout his skin. His eyes flickered yellow before his mouth opened, revealing a forked tongue.

Suddenly, in the blink of an eye, Donovan stood face to face with Kane, the undead prince, a terrifying mutation of both reptile and Umoyan appearing in a puff of purple smoke. Donovan lunged forward, but Kane swiftly seized him by the throat, preventing him from sinking his teeth into him. The monster emitted a shrill hiss before its face gradually melted away, blood dripping onto Kane's hands until only a skull remained.

"KANE," another voice echoed from afar.

He snapped his head around to find Cephas standing in the doorway, his face riddled with confusion.

"Release him, Kane," Cephas urged gently, his feeble hands raised in surrender. "Just let him go."

As Kane turned back, the skeletal figure vanished, and in its place was a terrified Donovan gasping for breath. The room had reverted to its former state, and the partygoers remained silent, their eyes fixed upon him. Some held their devices, capturing the unsettling spectacle. Finally, he released Donovan, who collapsed, struggling for air.

"Make way," a voice commanded, parting the crowd.

Cairo stumbled forward, accompanied by his Vadé and his close friend Sundiata.

"Kane, are you alright? Come on, bro, we out," Cairo said, guiding him through the party.

Amidst the fear, quiet anger, and confusion, the onlookers remained silent as Cairo, Vadé, and Sundiata escorted Kane through the gathering. He followed behind, consumed by embarrassment, until they finally emerged from the front doors and stepped back into the bustling streets of Mansa.

CHAPTER 3
THE OILS OF TRUTH
SERENITY

E xcuse me, Serenity and Princess Mariella," a short, innocent, dark-skinned girl ventured, weaving seamlessly through the busy sidewalk. Her eyes shimmered with hope as Serenity and Mariella gazed upon her, radiating a profound pride. "Could I get a picture with you?"

"And aren't you forgetting something?" Her mother stood a few inches behind her, a subtle reminder of familial support.

"Pa-pleeease?" the little girl added, accompanied by the most endearing gap-toothed smile Serenity had ever seen.

"Aww, you're simply adorable," Serenity cooed as she shifted her pink braids to the side, exposing her ochre-skinned shoulders, grace-fully lifting her silver dress to kneel and embrace the child. "What's your name, sweetheart?"

"Catori," the little girl whispered sheepishly.

"Come on, you stand in the middle, and make sure you smile big," Mariella encouraged, gently nudging her forward.

Overwhelmed with emotion, Catori's mother hastily retrieved her camera, capturing several precious moments of the gorgeous trio. As the camera clicked and laughter filled the air, a small crowd gathered, mirroring their excitement through their lenses.

"Um, Mariella, what's it like to be a princess?" Catori asked innocently.

"It's magical and full of hard work. You would be the perfect princess." Mariella remarked, rubbing Catori's cheek and making her smile.

"Serenity, do you wish you were a princess like Mariella?" Catori asked once the final photograph was taken.

"Oh no, that's not for me. Zion doesn't need me as the princess. One day, I'm going to go the nomad route and travel the galaxies," Serenity replied, her voice carrying a touch of self-doubt.

Catori flashed a look of surprise before her mother guided her away, vanishing into the crowd of lingering paparazzi. The girls passed by Shunny's famous lounge and opted to have a few oils to dull their nerves before the festival began. As they entered the lounge, Serenity observed her dear friend, Mariella, skillfully navigating the media's attention. She had always marveled at Mariella's innate ability to shape the narrative, garnering favor in the eyes of the press. Mariella was a pristine princess with an edge very few knew existed. She was a natural in front of the cameras, offering genuine and thoughtful responses to each question.

Dazzling in her emerald-colored strapless dress and coral heels, Mariella epitomized perfection. Her signature natural royal blue hair lay perfectly on her shoulders. After graciously fielding a few questions, she turned to Serenity, pulling her into the spotlight.

"Don't forget about my best friend," she playfully declared. "Isn't she beautiful? Make sure you get into this gorgeous silver Dinami original designed dress, honey."

Serenity could only respond with a sheepish half-smile as the cameras clicked away.

"Serenity, you look absolutely stunning. Those pink braids are styled perfectly! I have a few questions for you," a reporter called out.

Serenity glanced at Mariella, who silently urged her to answer.

"Did I hear you say to that little girl back there that you would like to be Queen of Zion one day?"

"I respect every member of the council, but honestly, I don't think I could ever do their jobs," Serenity replied, her humility clear and firm.

"You've been named the sneaky underdog in tonight's rankings. After training with not only the princes of Mansa, Kane, and Cairo, you were the surprise pick by Ganyah. Being part of the greatest Umoyan Nomad's group had to come with massive amounts of pressure, I assume?"

"I was grateful to be there and happy to all the people who supported this young girl from Zion." Serenity said humbly.

"I'm hearing you may even crack the top ten. How do you feel about where you might land tonight?"

"I did my best at the training isles, and I'm proud of what I could accomplish out there no matter where I land."

"You are so modest," the reporter smiled warmly, "Despite your words, I can envision you as a future Queen of Zion."

"I appreciate that, but like I said, I don't think it's my calling."

"Now that the training class has been back for a week, have you had the chance to speak with the newly crowned King and Queen of Zion? I'm very curious to hear your perspective on the riots erupting in your village over their decisions."

Serenity parted her lips to respond, but Mariella stepped forward before she could utter a word.

"You're a sneaky one, aren't you." Mariella joked, "That's all for now. You'll have the opportunity to interview once the rankings are out. But for now, we have somewhere to be. You guys be blessed by Gaia's light" With a graceful gesture, she blew a kiss to the reporters and gently pulled Serenity past the security guard patrolling the entrance to the lounge. Ignoring the public's whispers and stares, they entered the luxurious lounge.

"Don't you dare get tangled up in that mess surrounding the

Zion leadership! We are not about to let anything mess up this day," she warned.

The lounge inside was packed with Umoyans from various villages enjoying drinks, dancing to fast-paced music, or placing bets at the casino. Mariella led the way, skillfully maneuvering through the crowd towards the quieter and less crowded second floor. They quickly found a booth, and Mariella flagged down a waitress to order a few drinks.

"Isn't that Missy over there?" Mariella inquired, her finger pointing towards a lonesome figure occupying a table a few paces away.

"That sure is Motormouth," Serenity scoffed, her tone dripping with disdain.

"Don't do her like that," Mariella intervened. "She ain't that bad. You just can't tell her nothing you don't want repeated."

Reluctantly, Serenity trailed after Mariella, each step heavy with doubt. Missy sprang up from her seat, greeting them with a toothy smile. Cascades of long ebony hair adorned her shimmering silver dress, barely hugging her plump form and rich complexion. Missy clapped her hands excitedly as the duo drew near, extending her arms wide for an embrace. Mariella eagerly reciprocated, both erupting in laughter like a few carefree schoolgirls. Serenity mustered nothing more than a forced smile and a one-armed hug before she took her seat.

"Heyyyyy, if it ain't the dynamic divas!" Missy exclaimed; her smile so wide it almost concealed her eyes. "I see y'all had the good sense to come chill here. Shunny never lets the press in her lounge."

"That's why it's the best lounge in Mansa," Mariella chimed.

"What's going on, Serenity? Why are you so quiet over there? What's on your mind?" Missy asked.

"I won't lie; I'm just trying to get my nerves together before the rankings," Serenity responded.

"I know you're not worried; you did your thing out there; I'm a fan. You might end up being ranked the highest in the village. I hope you're ready for all the love that Zion is setting up to throw your way."

A short, mocha-skinned waitress with blonde tresses appeared, bearing a tray laden with drinks. Each cup brimmed with a peculiar, multicolored liquid. The waitress set down a pitcher filled with fuchsia-colored oils, causing Serenity's stomach to churn instantly. She could smell the potency of the concoction the moment it contacted the table.

"Y'all been catching wind of those riots over in Zion?" Missy interjected, sliding a cup in front of Serenity and Mariella before promptly downing half a cup of the vibrant, multicolored liquid. "Seems like things took a wild turn after we left."

Serenity took a hearty sip of the concoction, feeling the fiery sensation from the oils travel all the way down to the depths of her stomach.

"I've been staying in Zone G with Mariella since we've been back. I see what people are saying, though." Serenity remarked.

"Girl, it's a hot mess," Missy replied, her eyes wide with concern. "You ain't heard this from me, but folks out there ain't exactly on board with the new King and Queen's grand vision. They've got these cult fanatics parading around in robes, spewing nonsense left and right. Mind you, it's no secret they've been at odds with the council. The streets is saying a war is on the way if the council won't give them independence."

Serenity shook her head, trying to digest the troubling news, and she took another sip, drowning her thoughts in the potent oils. "Nobody has time for all of that," she muttered.

Mariella chimed in, her curiosity piqued, "I've heard whispers about this cult. Mars mentioned 'em."

Missy nodded gravely. "Mhm, those cultists got the whole city on edge. A lot of Umoyans believe they're behind the disappearances of low-born."

Mariella flagged down the waitress, her hand held high as a

signal for another drink. "Wait a minute," she urged, her voice low. "You're telling us Umoyans are vanishing?"

"In Zion, it's been a trend," Missy confessed in a hushed tone, leaning in even closer. "People tend to brush it off as nothing more than conspiracy, just a way to sling mud at the King and Queen, especially since most of 'em are low-born. I didn't buy it myself at first, but there's a search party scouring for Celeste right now between you and me—nobody's laid eyes on her since last night. As a matter of fact," she checked her watch, "I need to meet up with her mama soon. Poor woman's been a wreck."

"Are you serious?" Serenity's eyes widened in disbelief.

Missy nodded solemnly. "Yeah, they're trying to keep it hushed 'cause of the festival today. Who knows, maybe she's just laying low, trying to stay out of the way. I heard folks are downstairs, placing bets on her being the worst cadet in the class." Missy's tone dripped with disdain as she turned to the bustling casinos on the first floor.

Serenity followed her gaze, and her eyes met Shareeva's entrance into the lounge. A group of women accompanied Shareeva, their laughter echoing through the room, and many hailed from Zion. Serenity couldn't help but feel a sense of unease at the sight.

"And look at this one! I know she got something to do with this mess in Zion, too."

"What makes you think that?" Serenity inquired.

"Word on the street is she's practically set up shop in Zion these past few months. People think the new King and Queen are rallying behind her. You know folks in Zion want to distance themselves from anything remotely tied to Shakur," Missy explained, "The cults are spewing her old rhetoric after all."

"I hate the whole low-born thing. Why is anyone considered low just because they aren't connected to the sacred bloodlines? They really act like it's some kind of disease to have Shakur blood in you," Serenity snapped.

"Exactly! It's always something! You're blood this; you're family that! All of a sudden, Shakur isn't sacred; it's cursed because of some war that happened centuries ago! Half the people in Zion probably have a bit of Shakur blood in 'em. Not me, though, 'cause my great-grandmother was from Mansa, so you know, that's why I got all this hair," Missy chuckled. "Anyway, I gotta run, y'all. I'll catch you at the festival. Remember to be careful. This is the age of Apophis, and things have already clearly started going crazy." With a nod, she made her exit.

Serenity and Mariella bid their farewells to Missy, but Mariella's eyes remained fixed on Shareeva, and her entourage seated on the first floor.

"You know," Mariella began, her gaze still locked onto Shareeva, "I told Cairo about what happened with my brother. He was so messed up that night, Ren, he just kept saying stay away from the witch! Don't trust the witch! He begged me, high out of his mind."

Serenity nodded in understanding. "Shareeva has always rubbed me the wrong way since I was a child. She's always been creepy to me. I've never seen her in Zion, though."

"My parents have always hated her; she knows better than to be caught anywhere near that area."

"So, what do you think happened?" Serenity asked.

"I don't know. It's hard to ever know with him, but I know my brother. He seemed so convinced it's hard to think he was so far gone that Papa O finally had enough."

"Well, we don't know anything right now, so let's just have a good time till then." Serenity said, trying to lighten the mood.

"Yeah, you're right," Mariella muttered, frustration evident in her tone. She took another sip of her drink, her eyes never leaving Shareeva. "Did you ever get a chance to talk to Ganyah?"

Serenity nodded. "Yeah, same old Ganyah, giving his 'unlocked potential in you' speech."

"All these damn secrets" If he won't tell you why he chose you, at least explain why he didn't pick me to train alongside you and the Mansa princes?" Mariella took a strong sip of her drink and stared at

Shareeva's table as she sipped slowly until the cup was empty, to Serenity's shock.

Slamming her cup down, she rose from her seat, emboldened, "I'm sorry I have to say something. My twin is living in the streets and selling food out of an RV, but she's out here partying, acting like she doesn't know what's going on!"

Serenity quickly gathered their things as she followed behind Mariella, storming off in Shareeva's direction. Uncertain of what Mariella intended to say, Serenity knew that Shareeva was not one to engage in trivial conversations. Catching up to Mariella, she linked her arm with hers, showing solidarity as they approached the witch's table.

Sitting across from Shareeva was a fair-skinned woman with locks that flowed down her back that Serenity had never seen before. The other two women, cadets from Zion, halted her conversation, scrutinizing the two friends from head to toe. Serenity met their gaze, returning the same intensity before Shareeva finally broke the tension.

"Well, I wondered when you two would make your way over here. You sure were staring for quite some time," Shareeva remarked, a hint of amusement in her voice.

"We need to talk!" Mariella blurted out, her aggression obvious.

Shareeva chuckled at Mariella's outburst, calmly retrieving an extravagant purple and black cigarette holder. She inserted a small cigar into one end of the pipe and ignited it with a snap of her fingers. Taking a long drag, she exhaled a cloud of smoke into the air.

"Keiko, please make sure that task gets done while I take the opportunity to mentor these young ladies," Shareeva addressed her companion, her gaze remaining icy as she shifted her attention back to Mariella and Serenity.

Keiko nodded and excused herself from the table, leaving the three of them alone. Shareeva gestured for them to sit, adopting a more composed demeanor.

"Well, sit down, child. What can I do for the princess of Zone G, the *great* foundation of Umoya, and the gem of Zion," Shareeva said, turning her gaze to Serenity as she settled into her seat.

"What happened with my brother?" Mariella revealed, her frustration evident.

"Excuse me?" Shareeva scoffed, "Didn't your family say he was out of his mind on drugs? I'm confused."

"I know, my brother, he mentioned you! Why would he do that? Why would he make something like that up?"

"I'm sure if you knew what he said he saw, you'd have a different tone right now."

"There is nothing wrong with my tone," Mariella bellowed.

Shareeva paused, looking at Serenity as if awaiting her input. Even the Zion girls seemed to eagerly await the famed witches' response. Serenity remained stoic, waiting for Shareeva's reaction. Another drag, another puff of smoke, and finally, Shareeva broke her composed facade, bursting into laughter echoed by her team of followers, as she alternated her gaze between the two friends.

"Don't let your emotions turn you into a fool. Didn't they teach you that in the years' worth of training, y'all did? If you took the time to think, you'd realize I wouldn't be involved in anything in Zone G that your mother and father aren't privy to!" Shareeva stated firmly.

"With the Book of Apophis in your arsenal, anything is possible," Mariella suggested.

"ACCUSATIONS!" Shareeva exclaimed, pointing at Mariella, followed by a menacing cackle. "Your imagination is almost as wild as Mars. How could I have a book that no longer exists?"

"You think this is some sort of game?" Mariella barked, "I'm not playing with you!"

"No! You're clearly serious, but the real question is, what does Iris think about all of this?" Shareeva inquired.

"She's too caught up to worry about all of this, but I'm here to clear my brother's name," Mariella replied, holding her ground.

"*Right*. Correct me if I'm wrong, but wasn't it Osanyin himself who spread the rumors about your brother's *habits*?" Shareeva stated, slyly rubbing her nose. "I mean, come on, princess, are you going to accuse me of drugging him and making him hallucinate me in the forest of Zone G, killing one of the rarest animals in the forest? Chile, be serious."

"It must be the oils," one of the Zion girls snickered.

"Nobody was talking to either one of y'all, so keep it cute because Shareeva can't save you." Serenity spat boldly.

"Oop, is she talking to us?"

"Ladies, let me handle this," Shareeva said quickly, holding her hand up before they could reply, "They are here to learn just like you two should be doing."

"There's nothing I need to be learning from you," Serenity warned, her voice filled with caution.

"That's where you're wrong, my dear. The age of Apophis offers us opportunities to reach heights your little quest of ascension could never take you. This is the season born in the flames of his grace. Let him guide you and avoid the quest that will most likely lead to your deaths," Shareeva proposed.

"First of all, nobody has died on the quest in decades, so we're not worried. Secondly, you must be on Xenyd if you really think we're interested in whatever *you think* you have going on?" Mariella challenged.

"Be my guest, child. You two could have been something special, but the problem with both of you... well, that's a whole different conversation for another day," Shareeva stated, rising from her seat.

"Why not tell me now?" Serenity demanded, annoyed. "What is our problem?"

"How long do we have?" one of the Zion girls snickered.

Mariella seized the nearest cup of oils without hesitation and splashed it across the Zion cadet's face. A piercing shriek escaped her lips, and she fumbled to reach for a cup nearby. However, Serenity acted quickly, smacking the cup out of her hand and causing its contents to splatter across her dress.

Frustrated and disoriented, the Zion cadet launched a wild

swing, but Serenity skillfully evaded the strike and, with precision, mushed her back into a nearby bench. The other Zion cadet attempted to intervene, but Serenity's quick strikes forced her to stagger backward. As the third girl tried to blindside Serenity, Mariella executed a swift kick that knocked her to the ground, leaving the three Zion cadets in disarray.

"Enough!" Shareeva commanded, standing in between the girls as she turned to address the Zion cadets as they angrily regrouped militantly, positioning themselves behind Shareeva.

"Serenity! Mariella!" a familiar voice called out, cutting through the music from the entrance.

Serenity's heart sank as she turned and spotted Ganyah standing with a group of guards. He was the last person she wanted to witness the unfolding confrontation. Turning back, she discovered that Shareeva and the Zion cadets had somehow conveniently disappeared. She began walking toward Ganyah, attempting to compose herself discreetly and conceal the effects of the oils.

"How did he know we were here? Shouldn't he be preparing for the festival or something?" Mariella wondered, retrieving a pair of shades from her purse and putting them on, prompting Serenity to do the same.

"Who knows?" Serenity whispered as they approached.

Ganyah loomed over them, his expression stern and severe. Before she could speak, Ganyah raised his hand, gesturing them to remain silent.

"Security will escort you two straight to the stadium. We will discuss this later," Ganyah instructed, walking away.

With Mariella by her side, Serenity silently followed the security guards out of the lounge. She settled into the backseat of a hovercar and was left with more questions than the many Umoyan faces that lined the streets, hoping for a decent picture of the famous duo as they made their way to the stadium.

CHAPTER 4
A MOTHER'S QUANDARY
NEBI

T he resounding melodies of the United Umoyan band rang through the desolate stadium, infusing it with life, while the Queen of the realm perched on her crystallized throne, brimming with childlike excitement. Nebi, an extraordinary dancer, relished the homage paid to the four villages. Every corner of the land had witnessed auditions from musicians, flag bearers, acrobats, and dancers, all vying to form the grandest musical ensemble in Umoyan history. As the band concluded, Nebi applauded with all her might, her smile stretching from ear to ear.

"Well done! Well done!" she exclaimed; her enthusiasm peaked. "Everything was great. I need just a touch more energy from the horn players in the outro, but aside from that, well done!"

"Pardon me, your excellence," Manny spoke from behind.

Turning, Nebi maintained her smile as Manny quickly bowed, paying his respects. "Queen Nebi, there is something that requires your attention."

"What now?" Nebi muttered, attempting to conceal her irritation.

Fixing her gaze on the performance below, Nebi observed as Manny manipulated a few buttons on his wrist, revealing an image of Kane gripping the prince of Zion by the neck. Approaching Nebi, Manny captured her attention from the corner of her eye. Nebi raised her hand in response, causing the band to halt abruptly, assuming their positions until further instruction. The conductor hastened up the stadium stairs.

"Is everything alright, Your Highness?" the man asked, his face etched with worry.

"Everything is fine, Madiba," Nebi assured, pacifying the man's nerves. "Something has come up that demands my attention, and I refuse to miss a moment of your marvelous tribute. I only ask that the horns give a little more energy, and the dancer on the left must keep up with the steps. Other than that, I love what I'm seeing. We will run it again in a few minutes. Tonight, must be flawless!"

"I'm glad that the tribute meets your expectations, " Madiba replied, bowing so profoundly that his nose nearly grazed his knees.

"Ok, Manny, come with me," Nebi instructed, gesturing for Manny to follow her up the stadium stairs toward the skyboxes embedded in the arena's rim. "Do you know where my sons are now?"

"No, my Queen, but I can find them in no time," Manny affirmed.

"Good. There is still so much I need to do before the start of the festival," Nebi emphasized.

"Of course," Manny insisted.

"Make sure they stay out of trouble. Don't let them out of sight until they arrive at the festival. Between them and the council, it's always something!"

Nebi followed Manny out of the room, trailing the security detail along the stadium halls. The streets surrounding the stadium were barricaded, granting Nebi ample space to maneuver without encountering any heckling. Opening the door to her hover car, she noticed an older woman. She wore a faded green dress made in a style that Nebi hadn't seen since her youth, shuffling down the street alone. The security detail moved to approach her, but Nebi quickly intervened, electing to speak with the woman herself. As the woman drew nearer, her heart shattered into a thousand shards, witnessing the streams of tears tracing the woman's weathered face.

"Excuse me, do you need any help?" Nebi asked cautiously.

The woman remained silent, shoving her frail, wrinkled hand into her purse. After a few moments, she produced a photograph and held it up for Nebi to see.

"This is my son, Muldrow Mekari," the woman said, wiping her tears. "He is a good man, one of the hardest-working miners in Zion. He is my pride and joy."

"Did something happen to your son?" she asked gently, her concern evident.

"I haven't heard from my son in a few days now. I know my son, and this isn't like him," Ms. Mekari confessed.

"I'm sorry to hear that," Nebi offered, taking the photograph from Ms. Mekari and examining it more closely. "But if I may ask, why bring this here? You said you were from Zion, right?"

"Nothing is being done. So, I've searched and found several other low-borns have gone missing, just like my son! I took my information to the newly elected king and queen, and they may as well have shut the door in my face. Please! Help me find my Muldrow."

Nebi could feel the woman's pain stirring her soul, her heartache as a mother mirroring Ms. Mekari's. The innocence captured in Muldrow's photo only deepened Nebi's empathy.

"I will do everything I can to help you. I'm going to put you in contact with my assistant. He's amazing. We'll get to the bottom of this," Nebi assured.

Overwhelmed with relief, Ms. Mekari took Nebi into a warm embrace where she could feel her tears dampening Nebi's shoulder as her gratitude spilled forth. After the embrace, Nebi summoned one of the nearby guards and issued her instructions.

"Have Ms. Mekari escorted to the royal grounds. I will have Manny see her after he finds Kane and Cairo."

As the guards guided Ms. Mekari back into the building, Nebi glanced at her reflection in the mirror, contemplating the woman's words. Thoughts swirled in her mind as she pondered the plight of the missing Umoyans as well as the dismissive attitude of Zion's new leaders. Unable to contain her thoughts, she jumped into her car and activated the partition in the backseat, seeking a moment of privacy while contemplating Ms. Mekari's words.

When the hover car pulled into the office parking lot, anticipation filled her heart; seeing the council members' vehicles lined up in their designated spots was welcoming. Accompanied by the guards, she entered the building, greeted by an Umoyan woman at the front desk, whose warm welcome guided them to the meeting room. Nebi took notice of Azazel and Mara's nonchalant demeanor and made a point of engaging with the familiar faces first, allowing the pleasantries of her alliances to warm her up enough to address the unbothered couple.

Once she was ready, Nebi procured two drinks and approached Azazel and Mara. She observed their reactions with each step, her intuition sharpened by years of politics. None of them acknowledged her until she cleared her throat and placed the cups on the desk before them, interrupting their conversation.

"Good afternoon, Azazel, Mara," Nebi greeted, her tone polite but laced with a subtle undercurrent of disdain. "I'm pleased to see you both here."

Azazel, a mocha-skinned man with a million-dollar smile, rose from his seat and extended a hand.

"Good afternoon, Queen Nebi. Thank you for hosting us."

Mara, a conniving tan-skinned woman, stood up and extended her hand. "My husband and I are ecstatic. I've always found the festival to be...*primitive fun.*"

Nebi flashed a sarcastic smile, hoping to mask her true sentiments. "Well, come join us, and let us begin. I want to ensure everyone can enjoy all Mansa offers before the show starts."

"After you," Mara replied, following Nebi toward the roundtable at the center of the oval-shaped room.

Nebi's eyes fell upon the empty chair beside hers as everyone gathered around the table. It would have been her husband's seat, a poignant reminder of his absence. Taking her seat, Nebi suppressed any lingering emotions, focusing on the tasks.

However, Mara couldn't resist a comment. "Alo won't be joining us? Doesn't tradition call for all of us to be here?"

"The King is in the meditation chamber with the shamans, gaining his strength for the journey into the spirit realm," Shunny snapped.

"My regards," Mara responded, "We wish him the best. He doesn't appear to be himself of late. We wish the Gods grant him strength," her words accompanied by a whisper to her husband. Azazel smiled and patted her hand, conveying their shared secret.

"We appreciate your concern. I assure you the King is fine. Let us begin," Nebi announced, clearing her throat and swallowing every negative impulse she had to respond, determined to rise above the bitterness emanating from the leaders of Zion. "First off, I am happy to see each of your faces. These last few months have been challenging, yet we are still here, together, ready to celebrate the future of our realm. If you direct your attention to the table screen, you will find the agenda for today. Let's address the needs of our realm."

Shunny rose from her seat, assuming her role in the proceedings. "Hiram has produced its largest yield of metals in history. Expect the delivery to the other villages as soon as everyone returns home."

"Thank you, Shunny and Safan, for your invaluable contributions to the realm," Nebi expressed her gratitude. "How is the educational outreach program progressing?"

"Queen Mother, we are proud to report that the educational outreach agenda is in full force, resulting in a doubling of the graduation rate in each village," Safan shared, his voice resonating with pride.

Osanyin, standing up, cleared his throat before speaking. "The village of Zion has harvested enough to feed the realm three times over. Of course, we would have more if we had more liquid maisha to fuel harvest collectors, but the Gods have blessed us.

The council's attention shifted toward the leaders of Zion. Azazel stood up, adjusting his tailored suit before addressing the gathering.

"It is no secret that there have been challenges since we assumed leadership in Zion. We acknowledge the concerns voiced by many and validate each one of them. However, we believe in our resolve and ask for a little more time to meet the village's obligations in providing liquid Maisha and resources for the realm. We have faced setbacks in completing our new district, and our efforts and resources have been redirected to resolve these issues."

"This is your sixth time unable to fully meet the obligations. Forgive me if I'm assuming, but it appears that you don't recognize the urgency of the situation," Nebi began coldly. "Each time you cannot fulfill your obligations, the rest of the villages are affected. Liquid Maisha is the lifeblood of the realm. The rest of the realm doesn't produce nearly as much liquid maisha as Zion," Nebi replied.

"I can assure you that we recognize the severity of the situation and vow to work to resolve our issues."

"Something has to be done. I hear more about your village seeking independence than I am solutions to help solve the crisis you create every time you can't meet your quotas," Shunny added.

"First, I can assure you that there have never been any official conversations about departing from the council," said Azazel, "I'm afraid those are nothing, but rumors spread by those that don't favor us."

"It's been all over the press that these rumors are more than just rumors," Osanyin added.

"Last time I checked, Osanyin, you have more ties to the press than anyone." Mara shot at him, "It's best if we just ignore those rumors and block them out."

"Just like the rumors of missing Umoyans in your village, right?" Nebi sternly introduced into the conversation.

"Missing Umoyans?" Azazel scoffed, slightly confused, "I have no idea what you are talking about."

"I figured you'd say that. I spoke with a woman today, and she alleges you slammed the door in her face when she tried to bring the situation to your attention. "

Alleged," Mara exclaimed, "Meaning that you have no basis to the claim besides the word of some mystery low-born woman from the corner of the realm."

"You literally run that corner of the realm; do you hear yourself? As alleged as the claims may be, it would behoove you to look into the claims before you dismiss her based on your own ignorance," Shunny added coldly.

"Ignorance?" Mara scoffed as Azazel rubbed her hand, calming her down.

"An investigation needs to take place immediately," Safan suggested.

"We will surely investigate, but I assure you there is no need to assume the worst. Let alone throw out insults; I'm sure there is a simple explanation for all this." Azazel added, calming the room down.

"I appreciate your diplomacy, Azazel, and hopefully, your actions match your words," Nebi ordered.

"We will do everything we can," Azazel insisted.

"The investigations have already begun," Nebi said, watching Mara shift uncomfortably in her seat. Azazel seemed taken aback by her words, "My assistants are already investigating the woman's claims. She sought me out, and I couldn't find it in me to turn her away. I will surely keep you in the loop and work alongside whomever you are comfortable with on your behalf to put these rumors to bed before they grow legs."

"All that without consulting us first?" Mara retorted, "We can handle our own investigation. This matter doesn't need the attention of the entire council."

"Agreed," said Azazel, finally taking his seat.

"The woman came to me personally. So, I will conduct the investigation, but I give you my word you will be involved throughout this process." Nebi insisted, "Consider the matter closed.

Azazel and Mara exchanged uneasy glances, aware of Nebi's firm stance. The council members followed suit, the tension in the room so thick that you could cut it with a knife. Nebi closed the meeting, dismissing the council members to enjoy the festivities. Azazel and Mara wasted no time bidding their farewells and leaving the room. Before the door closed, Shunny stormed over to Nebi, her anger evident as a throbbing vein pulsed on her forehead.

"Who do they think they are? I don't know how they could have been elected with those attitudes."

"I agree, Queen Mother," Safan concurred. "Things haven't been this bad in the council since the days of the war, and I still have nightmares of the things we were forced to do. We have to fix this mess before we end up back there."

"I will bring them to the light," Nebi vowed. "Do not worry."

"If not, then we will bring them to their knees. I don't have the energy for another war, Nebi," Shunny questioned with concern.

"Have a little faith," Nebi replied, offering a wink.

"I have faith in you," Shunny assured. "It's them I don't have any faith in."

Nebi shook her head, amused, as Osanyin and Iris approached to bid their farewells to the rest of the council.

"I noticed you were unusually quiet, Iris," Shunny said, her tone laced with shade.

"The council knows my stance on the new leadership in Zion. I wish Ivonne and Levi were still on the throne. Ivonne wouldn't have stepped down if the Gods had seen fit for Levi to overcome his illness. Gods rest her soul, first her child, then her husband. I see why the poor woman couldn't go on any longer," Iris lamented.

"Get them in line, Nebi, or things will get ugly around here. I don't believe for a second that those fools didn't have official conversations about leaving the council and seeking independence. Now, we have this missing Umoyan business to think about. What the hell is going on over there?"

"They are bleeding us. They know that our lives would become very difficult without their Liquid Maisha. We need to do something!" Shunny added.

"And it will," Nebi assured.

"Come on, Safan, let's go, please. We have two more outfit changes before we have to be on stage."

"See you all at the festival, and good luck," Nebi concluded, bidding farewell to the remaining council members.

As Nebi exited the room, she headed toward her hover car when she received a phone call from Manny. Excitement filled her as she answered and awaited his holographic image to appear before her.

"Good evening, my queen. I'm in route to the princes right now. They're together and heading downtown. Vadé and Sundiata are accompanying them."

"Thank you, Manny! Do not let them out of your sight. No pit stops."

"Copy."

"One more thing, Manny. I need you to look into something for me."

"Anything for you. Where should I begin?"

"I want you to speak with a woman currently on the grounds. Ms. Mekari possesses some intriguing information I wish to address before it becomes too much of a problem."

"It will be my pleasure."

"And, Manny, keep this information strictly confidential. No one should know what you uncover until I understand what we are dealing with."

"Understood, my queen. Is there anything else?"

"No, that will be all, dear. I'll see you soon," Nebi concluded, ending the call.

As Manny's holographic image dissipated, Nebi found herself alone in the car, staring at the swarming crowds approaching the stadium for the realm's grandest show. The joyous reactions she witnessed warmed her heart, but her true fulfillment would come when her sons walked across that stage as esteemed Umoyan men.

CHAPTER 5
HE ON THAT STUFF
KANE

And you're just telling me all this now?" Kane scoffed, shaking his head. "I told y'all that Zion was acting strange since we got back from training! Now you're telling me they are going."

"So, is that why you were gripping up their Prince back there?" Cairo asked, "What in the name of the Gods was that?"

Embarrassed, Kane just turned out of the window.

"Talk to us, bro!" Cairo barked, "He said something to you, didn't he?"

"I.... just reacted ok!" Kane spat, "Something weird is going on with me, and I tripped out. Now it's going to be everywhere, and Umoyans all over the realm are going to add more fuel to this Mansa versus Zion mess."

"Calm down; what do you mean something is going on with you?" Cairo asked.

"I spoke to Dad about it earlier; it's nothing I can't handle. I just had a moment."

"Listen, no need to trip. I don't like Donovan anyway. That's

Maaku's best friend, so it doesn't matter what happened at the end of the day," Cairo responded with a shrug.

"Yeah, chill, cuz," Vadé cautioned. "We still don't know what this beef is really about."

Kane's expression remained stern. "That doesn't matter; If Zion pushes for independence, that is going an act of war."

Sundiata chimed in, his voice tinged with concern. "What's the realm without liquid maisha? They could cripple the realm if they start acting stingy."

"That won't happen," Cairo stated flatly.

Kane, however, remained skeptical. "I don't know. It's the age of Apophis. Things have been pretty chaotic since we returned. Have y'all been keeping up with what's happening with that Zealot cult?"

"Oh, you mean Shareeva's little prodigies? I told y'all what Mars told me," Vadé added.

Kane continued, "Yeah, but does anyone actually know what Mars claimed he saw?" He observed his brother and friends as they shook their heads.

Cairo raised an eyebrow. "Does it really matter? We can't pretend Mars is the most reliable source. I mean, he's cool, and that's my guy, but come on."

Kane countered, "He's crazy, but he's not that far gone. Don't you find it strange that no one knows what he saw?"

"Whatever it was, it must've been crazy. The only Umoyans who heard his story were his parents, and they kicked him out, saying he was high out of his mind," Vadé interjected.

"He be on that stuff," Cairo added with a shrug.

Kane, however, pressed further, "Are you sure that's all he said?"

Vadé recollected, "All he said was that we can't trust Shareeva. I tried to get more out of him, but he kept alluding to her trying to bring an end to the realm." Vadé paused, his voice lowering. "He was really skittish. You know how he is all extra suspicious of every Umoyan now."

Kane pondered the situation silently, feeling at a loss. He glanced at Manny through the rearview mirror, catching his watchful gaze.

"Manny, you've been working with our family since we left for training, right?" Kane asked, his voice filled with a blend of determination and curiosity.

"Yes, sir," Manny replied nervously, trying to navigate the delicate conversation.

"Well, does any of this make sense to you? You must know something," Kane inquired, hoping for additional insight.

"Well, there haven't been any reports or evidence regarding Shareeva and any forbidden activities. She's been seen in Zion a few times but has remained, for the most part, in accordance with her banishment. I understand you guys have somewhat of a connection with Prince Mars, but we must consider the facts," Manny explained, trying to provide a balanced perspective.

"I'm with you, Manny," Cairo said, supporting Manny's viewpoint.

"There is *some* credence to postponing this year's festival and quest behind the mishaps of Zion. Unfortunately, their unforeseen setbacks have thrown the festivities into question. Luckily, your mother and the rest of the council worked it out and made today's festival possible."

"So, that's what you must've heard, Vadé," Cairo concluded, finally understanding the situation.

"But what's really going on in Zion? What are these setbacks?" Kane probed, eager to uncover the truth.

"They're expanding their village and building a new district. Their leaders claim they've faced several mishaps that have caused them to fall short of providing liquid Maisha for the realm. The problem is their setbacks have a ripple effect on the rest of the villages. Each village depends on one another, so when one struggles..."

"We all struggle," Kane finished, reciting the old Umoyan mantra.

"Looks like I was right, bro," Cairo stated, reaffirming their doubts, "This is all some kind of misunderstanding."

Kane shook his head, a sense of unease creeping over him.

"Kane, I know that look, bro. We're already in trouble..." Cairo began, his tone filled with caution.

"Your brother is right," Sundiata cautioned.

"Listen, I feel like we should talk to Mars and find out what he saw that night. He'd tell us the truth if we asked Cairo, and you know it!" Kane declared, determined to seek the truth.

"Nah, bro, we have to get to the festival on time. Otherwise, that's all anyone will talk about," Cairo argued, concerned about their reputation, "Mommy is already pissed."

"Yeah, Kane, we can figure all that out after the festival is over," Vadé added.

We can't just ignore this. We have to figure out what he saw that night! When I spoke with Pop earlier, he told me these feelings I'm having are callings from the Gods. He told me to listen, and I'm listening." Kane insisted, refusing to back down.

"What callings?" Cairo questioned.

Manny interrupted, sensing the urgency in their voices. "If it eases your nerves, Prince Kane, we'll pass Mars's food truck soon. I can take you there and ensure you make it to the festival on time; you'll only have a few minutes to spare. But we can make it work," Manny proposed, offering a solution.

"Come on, Manny, not you too," Cairo protested, frustrated by the turn of events.

"There it goes, thank you, Manny. That's what I needed," Kane said, acknowledging Manny's support with a half-smile, "If it's nothing, then we won't be there long, but my gut is telling me that there is something more, bro. You have to —"

"If you say that I have to trust you, I'm going to punch you right in your throat," Cairo warned, "Let's just go and get it over with."

Manny picked up the pace, skillfully maneuvering through side streets and navigating the traffic, heading toward Mars's location on the east side of town. Cairo, Sundiata, and Vadé occupied themselves by scrolling through social media while Kane anxiously observed the passing scenery, his stomach churning with the weight of time ticking away.

When the car finally stopped, Kane swiftly exited the vehicle, making a beeline for Mars's truck. Among the many vendors selling festival-themed merchandise, Mars's truck stood out with its prominent signage, "Mad Max," blinking in vibrant colors. The forest green truck was decorated with teal accents in the form of flowers and herbs and spanned almost half a block. One end of the truck served as a restaurant with a serving window and an extended roof, while the other end showcased mannequins donning Mad Max apparel.

As they approached the food truck, Kane's nerves intensified, unsure of how much he wanted Mars to reveal. Suppressing his doubts, Kane raised his fist to knock on the door when a raspy voice came down from above.

"Well, well, well. Look at who we have here?"

Peeking out from a hatch in the ceiling of the truck was Mars. He quickly pulled himself up and slid down the truck's roof, landing before the gang, tall and lanky, clumsily dressed with only one arm in his green work shirt, jet-black jeans, and blue sneakers. He tied his hair into a loose ponytail, attempting to tame its wildness.

"To what do I owe the pleasure of royalty at my door? Figured your parents would be telling you to stay far away from me by now."

"Nah, it ain't like that at all!" said Kane, "With everything happening, we never got a chance to catch up with you since we returned," Kane began. "We've heard a lot about your situation, so we came to make sure you're okay and show our faces."

"I appreciate that. It means a lot that you came out of your way," Mars replied gratefully.

"So, are you living out of this truck now?" Kane asked.

"Ever since Osanyin kicked me out, yeah. I go wherever the business takes me," Mars explained.

"What time do you plan on coming to the festival? I know Mariella will be hyped when she sees you arrive to watch her get ranked."

"I love my twin. I always knew she would be great, but I want nothing to do with that festival or, respectfully, the entire council," Mars expressed, his tone tinged with bitterness.

"Why all that?" Kane asked, intrigued by Mars's perspective.

Mars chuckled, reaching into his pocket to retrieve what remained of a rolled-up joint. He leaned against the truck, lighting it up and taking a long drag, exhaling a cloud of smoke.

"I didn't want to say anything, but there's so much the council likes to keep hidden *for the sake of the realm*," Mars said, his voice laced with a sense of secrecy.

"You're talking about that night in the forest, right?" Kane pressed, urging Mars to continue. "What happened to you that night?"

Mars glanced around, ensuring they were free of eavesdropping ears, before taking a few more puffs from his joint, gathering his thoughts before resuming.

"Things you'd think only happen in nightmares, Kane. I honestly shouldn't have been out there in the first place," Mars confessed.

"Why were you in the forest at night anyway?" Cairo asked, curious to uncover the truth.

"Osanyin banned me from access to a lot of my supplies back home. So now I have to sneak around the village like some sort of criminal. He can't bother me in other villages as much, but that hasn't stopped his little spies from coming here to tell him my every move." Mars retorted, bitterness tainting his words.

Kane, taken aback by Mars' accusations, responded, "I didn't know."

"Yeah, well, ever since I refused the oh-so-sacred quest, that man can barely even look at me. He told me that I'm no better than the rest of the fools who are afraid to evolve into what the Gods had ordained for us," Mars explained, his voice heavy with resentment.

"That's messed up," Vadé interjected softly. "If you don't want to take the quest, that should be your choice."

"Not when you're the prince," Kane added, "Certain titles come with certain responsibilities whether you want them or not."

"Five of my brothers and sisters died on that quest. I'm sorry if I chose to deal with the safer side of maisha, like your family," said Mars, pointing at Sundiata, "Nobody in the entire realm talks down on them for not taking the quest, and they helped revolutionize the use of maisha!"

"I feel you on that," Sundiata empathized.

"Maisha is why we have everything we have now. The crystal's energy powers every fiber of the realm. On the real, y'all wouldn't even be able to take the quest if you didn't mine raw maisha as a part of your training. That enchanted forest you have to travel through would've sucked the life force right out of you in seconds without it." Mars elucidated passionately.

"What exactly where you looking for in the forest?" Kane asked.

"Solar Daisy, my friend," Mars replied, taking another drag from his joint. Half amused at the bewildered expressions on Kane and Cairo's faces, he remarked, "I'm guessing by the look on your faces you have no idea what that is?"

Kane turned to Cairo, seeking any hint of recognition, yet he could offer nothing but a perplexed shrug. "I'm guessing it's some kind of flower," Kane ventured.

"Yes, this plant possesses extraordinary properties, inducing psychedelic effects. Once I perfect the dosage, it shall revolutionize our realm," Mars asserted, tapping the plant's design adorning his truck. "Anyway, these babies are only native to a certain place in the forest of Zone G. I snuck past security, snuck through the village, and hiked it through the forest in the dead of night. I get to the patch, collect what I need, and make my way out when I hear this crazy noise," Mars recounted.

"What did it sound like?" Kane queried, hanging onto every word.

"'Sounded like chanting," Mars replied, his voice carrying the weight of uncertainty. "I didn't know the language, but I saw a black unicorn shackled to a tree by two weirdos dressed in black robes. The unicorn struggled and thrashed, desperately trying to free itself, while they chanted around a fire. Suddenly, the flames started turning purple, growing taller than me."

"How did they get their hands on a black unicorn?" Cairo asked.

Mars took another extended pull from his joint, shrugging nonchalantly.

"The black robes had to be the Zealots," Sundiata added, "Did they have creepy-looking demon-faced masks?"

"Oh, so you know about the Zealots?" Mars inquired, "They're dangerous."

"Why do you say that? What happened?" Kane inquired eagerly.

"Well, that's when I saw your aunt, Shareeva, emerging from the flames," Mars proclaimed, pointing his smoking joint toward Kane and Cairo before indulging in another drag. "Wildest thing I've ever seen, hands down. It was like she stepped out of a portal or something holding a black book."

"A portal inside the flames?" Kane attempted to comprehend.

"I'm just telling you what I saw," Mars defended. "She stepped out, and the weirdos in the robes kneeled before her like she was some kind of God or something. Then, she slowly crept up to the black unicorn, whispered something to it, stared at it for a second, and then took a blade to its neck."

"This is sick," Cairo interjected, his voice filled with revulsion. "What the hell kind of ritual is this?"

"The blood of the black unicorn is probably the most potent magical essence in the realm, and she was drinking it, bro. There was so much that she was bathing in the stuff. I'm talking bout' rubbing it all over her skin like she was enjoying it while the ones in the hooded robes chanted into the night.

"Man, I'm done with Shareeva!" Cairo exclaimed, "Do y'all hear what he's saying?"

"Oh, it gets crazier."

"What do you mean it gets crazier?" said Vadé, shaking his head in disbelief.

"After slaying the unicorn, the hooded figures unveiled their faces, took out their blades, and ended their lives one by one while Shareeva uttered weird incantations, using her magic to elevate the lifeless bodies and cast them into the purplish flames," Mars paused momentarily to indulge in another puff of his joint. "That's when I heard the bodies being ripped apart."

"What was Shareeva doing?" Kane queried, his nerves tingling.

"She was cackling like a manic laughter before using magic to hoist the unicorn's carcass just before the flames. A strange creature emerged, extending its arm, and dragged the lifeless body into the inferno until it vanished," Mars described.

Kane could feel his heartbeat thumping so hard that it reverberated through the soles of his feet as he recollected his visions, "And what did that creature look like?"

"I couldn't tell what it was. The thing never left the fire, but anything that can grab an adult unicorn with one arm isn't something I want problems with. I didn't have the stomach to listen to the body get ripped apart, and I sure as hell didn't want to be next, so I bolted. " Mars concluded.

"I would have done the same thing," Cairo affirmed. "Actually, I wouldn't have even been out there."

"I went back and told Mom and Osanyin, but you know how that played out."

As outlandish as the story may sound, Kane discerned a sincerity in Mars' eyes. He pondered whether he should trust the words of a known drug addict. Yet, there was an authenticity about Mars that resonated within him. Mars was either the most skilled liar he had ever met, or worse, his words held truth, spelling genuine danger upon their realm.

"If you were smart, you'd join the Underground with me," Mars urged. "We're escaping the nightmares that your council keeps locked away."

"The Underground?" Kane inquired; his curiosity piqued.

"We are everywhere and nowhere," Mars teased, beginning to elaborate, "It's a lot of funny business going on in Zion, and all the chaos is spilling all over the realm."

"Like what?" Vadé asked.

"You mean outside of the creepy rituals, spikes in the use of dark energy, beef in the council, and missing Umoyans?"

"I knew it was bad, but all that?" Kane said, shaking his head.

"I ran into a woman named Ms. Mekari on my travels selling food, and she put me down with her son Muldrow and a group of Umoyans —"

"Muldrow?" Kane stammered, his heart plummeting to the floor at the casual mention of his nightmare.

"Yeah, he was one of the first to start talking about the Zealots and went missing, spawning the Underground.

Kane couldn't believe what he was hearing. He could picture Muldrow's heroics like a movie in his head as Mars continued.

"It's like a brotherhood. We are the—"

Before Mars could finish his sentence, a thunderous bang erupted from the truck's rear, cutting him off abruptly.

Emerging from around the corner, Donovan, Maaku, Ian, and Iggy arrived boisterously and unapologetically. Mars swiftly crushed his joint into ashes and cast it to the ground.

"What the hell do y'all want?" Kane snapped, his anger palpable.

"I thought I heard the jaded Prince's voice. I just didn't think you'd have the nerve to be outside after that stunt you pulled at your trainer's house," Donovan taunted, his challenging tone hanging in the air. "How about you try to finish what you started right here right now!"

"Yeah, what's up now, Cairo?" Ian taunted; his bravado unchecked. "You got lucky earlier, but if everyone weren't around, I would've—"

"You would've what?" Cairo interrupted, stepping forward to meet the challenge.

"Chill out, Cairo," Mars cautioned, trying to mediate.

"Stay out of this, Mad Mars," Maaku teased.

"You should know your place," Donovan added, his tone dripping with condescension.

Mars swiftly intervened, his voice carrying a warning. "You should also know that your little royal titles won't protect you here. Watch your mouth and keep it moving."

"Why should I respect someone who doesn't even have the respect of his village?" Donovan fired back, his taunts escalating. "Do yourself a favor, climb back into your little house, and stay out of this. Kane thought it was amusing to try and embarrass me in front of all the guardians. What's up now?"

Kane sighed, realizing further words were futile. He stepped forward, prepared to answer the challenge, much to Cairo's delight. However, Mars swiftly blocked his path with his arm.

"Nah, y'all, go ahead and get to the festival," Mars declared firmly. "If they want trouble, I'll give them all they want."

Before Kane could protest, Mars raised his fist high, commanding attention. The surrounding Umoyans stopped in their tracks, and Umoyans emerged from vending trucks, stalls, and the streets. A hushed tension filled the air as all eyes focused on Donovan, Maaku, Ian, and Iggy.

"Come on, Donovan. Not here," Maaku whispered urgently, taking in the overwhelming numbers around them.

"You're right," Donovan agreed, wearing a mocking smirk as he raised his fist. "Let's go."

Mars lowered his fist, and the bystanders returned to their business, allowing the group to pass through the street. Manny's voice cut through the tension, signaling the crew to retreat to the car. Cairo, Sundiata, and Vadé headed back, but as Kane moved to follow, Mars grabbed his arm.

"Listen, I know you're not all caught up in the front the council likes to put on, and the Underground could use y'all for what's coming. It's the age of Apophis now," Mars whispered, his voice low and intense. "And from what I saw in that forest that night, a war brewing will change everything as we know it. Those yellow eyes I saw in the flames haunt me to this day."

"Yellow eyes?" Kane's heart sank as he made the connection. "You mean the—"

"Shhh," Mars interrupted, nodding gravely. "I think they're back. You need to be cautious around your aunt and the Zealots. They're messing with things that could cost you more than your life."

Kane nodded in understanding, shook Mars's hand, and then trotted back to the car, silently accepting the challenge. "I've got to be ready," he thought resolutely. "I will be ready."

CHAPTER 6
I JUST CAN'T WAIT TO BE...
CAIRO

F ocus, tonight, you become number one," Cairo whispered to himself, determined to block out the numerous distractions that had besieged his mind. He knew that this was the moment he had long yearned for. Cairo's focus intensified as he gazed into the dim tunnels, shrouded in crimson lasers and swirling smoke. Outside, the crowd's excitement reverberated in the background.

Turning to Kane, he asked, "You good, bro?"

Though struggling with the weight of his own nerves from the impending event, Kane replied, "Yeah. Let's get this over with."

Their leader for the event, Madiba, barked out orders, commanding the attention of the cadets. With his authoritative voice, he sliced through the mounting anticipation as he moved to the front of their marching formation. "Look alive, cadets! Look alive! Here we go!"

With a synchronized precision that only well-trained cadets could achieve, they followed Madiba into the tunnel. The torchlight cast flickering shadows along the tunnel's walls, lighting their path as they ventured deeper. They came to a halt as Madiba stood before the colossal metal door, its centerpiece adorned with the Mansa sigil.

The door split down its center, allowing the full force of the light show and screams from the Umoyans awaiting the reveal. Madiba began the march, leading the cadets into the expansive stadium, which was brimming with an audience that appeared to feature almost every Umoyan in the realm. Cairo's keen ears detected faint boos emanating from the Zion section. He dismissed it as the response of some overindulgent Zion audience members.

The colossal floating screen projected the image of the royal council, who were positioned before their ornate thrones, embedded within a crystal structure that reached the heights of the royal palace at the center stage. The cadets representing the other three villages had already settled at the round tables and booths scattered before the main stage.

A substantial floating platform approached, and the Mansa cadets ascended it for their ceremonial lap around the stadium. Cairo beamed his million-dollar smile, encouraging the entire audience to rise to their feet.

"MANSA! MANSA! MANSA!" the crowd roared, displaying their unwavering support.

Nevertheless, as the platform glided past the Zion section, Cairo was startled to hear the faint boos growing louder. He exchanged a surprised look with Kane. Amid the commotion, security personnel were escorting a group of overly enthusiastic Zion supporters out of the stadium. The tension in the crowd was palpable, and Cairo began to wonder if they would even make it to the end of the rankings in this highly charged atmosphere.

The platform finally descended, and Madiba led the cadets with unwavering pride to the seating area to the tune of applause by the Mansa section, refusing to be unheard. Representatives from the other villages also stood and respectfully applauded as they took their places.

Cairo guided Kane to the roundtable where Vade, Mariella,

Serenity, and Sundiata had gathered, securing a spot beside them. Each table was adorned with opulent black tablecloths adorned with golden embellishments, and they featured delectable finger foods and a pitcher of water at their centers.

As Cairo settled down beside Mariella, he couldn't help but feel a rush of butterflies as her sweet scent enveloped him. Despite his best efforts to conceal his emotions, Mariella leaned in for a hug, and Cairo felt his heart nearly burst in his chest.

"Hey, Roro. You look handsome," Mariella whispered with a soft smile as she settled into her seat.

Cairo's nerves got the best of him, and he stammered, "Uh, hey, Mari." He scratched the back of his head, captivated by the emerald depths of her gaze. "Gaia herself could not rival your beauty."

"Ahhhhh!" Vade and Sundiata exclaimed, throwing up their arms.

"Relax," Cairo chuckled, addressing his friends before the teasing could escalate.

"Thank you, Roro, even though I'm sure I'm not the first girl you've used that line on," Mariella teased.

"Mariella, you're the only one I want to have by my side in my Kingdom," Cairo replied earnestly.

"Well, stop letting me hear about you and these other girls, and there may be room for you in my Queendom," Mariella shot back, her gaze locking with Cairo's, a challenge hidden in her eyes.

Cairo returned the gaze. "So, you're telling me none of these guys out here have your attention?"

"Anyway," Mariella said, swiftly changing the subject and looking back at Nebi, "Your mother surely didn't pull any punches putting all of this together." She marveled at the grandeur surrounding them.

"She put her all into it despite not having everything she needed. A true queen," Serenity added, paying homage to Nebi from her seat.

Cairo, still curious, asked, "Speaking of not having everything she needed, what's up with the people from Zion booing us? Didn't our section cheer for y'all?"

"You know Zion feels like they have something to prove! Hell, we even had a little run-in with your aunt and some girls from Zion earlier," Serenity explained, "I feel like they are only tolerating me right now because of how I performed in training, but normally, they always got something to say about always being underneath of y'all."

"Hold on, our aunt. Do you mean Shareeva?" Kane asked.

"Yeah, and her little cult of Zion girls," Mariella said, taking a sip of her drink.

"So, they managed to get into a fight, and not one person has a video of it, thank Osanyin." Vade teased.

"Must be nice," Sundiata joked.

"So Shareeva was with some girls from Zion? Why?" Kane asked, ignoring the jokes, fully enthralled in putting the pieces together.

"It was bizarre," Serenity added. "She wanted us to join her but wouldn't say for what. I don't know what she's on, but this is one girl from Zion she won't be fooling with her nonsense."

"It's not surprising she has people from Zion following her. You know how you girls are." Mariella said, nudging Serenity jokingly.

"I don't know, *princess,* how are we?" Serenity fired back, chuckling.

"Some would say you guys are...fierce," Mariella responded, trying to find the word.

"Rude," Vade added.

"Aggressive," Sundiata quickly threw in.

"Troublemakers," Cairo finished.

"Now, don't do Zion like that. Shareeva is related to three people at this table, and that's all I'll say about that! Secondly, no one from Zion has ever burned an entire village down with the power of the sun," Serenity sarcastically shot as she took a sip of her drink.

"Ooooohhhh," Vade and Sundiata said, instigating the situation.

"Chill out, Ren. I know you're not one of those people to follow behind Shareeva. It's just been a lot of talk of her being in and out of Zion recently," Kane responded, addressing Serenity.

"Enough, cuz," Vade interjected, attempting to put an end to the heavy conversation. "We spent a whole year in training and fighting amongst one another for an entire year! We all have probably done enough to earn top-ten potential. Can we just enjoy our flowers, please?"

Before Cairo could part his lips and agree, the conversation was interrupted as a fight broke out in the Zone G section of the stadium. The jumbotron then captured another Zion protester, revealing clashing with a group of Zone G individuals.

Cairo glanced up at the stage, where his parents were observing the commotion. In a bid to regain control of the situation, a tall, lanky man with a blue and gold Hiram sigil walked up and seized the microphone.

"LADIES AND GENTLEMEN, PLEASE HAVE SOME RESPECT! SETTLE YOURSELF!" she bellowed, waiting for the crowd to settle at the sound of her voice, "THAT'S MORE LIKE IT! NOW RISE, AND PUT YOUR HANDS TOGETHER FOR THE KING OF ALL UMOYA, KING ALO!"

The announcement settled the stadium and diverted everyone's attention to King Alo as he stood from his seat and kissed Nebi on the cheek before taking his time as he shakily descended to the stage on a floating platform from the magnificent crystal structure. Cairo snuck another nervous look at Kane as they witnessed their father try to conceal his struggle as he navigated the stage.

He cleared his throat before he addressed the rowdy crowd, "PLEASE, PLEASE, BE SEATED, MY PEOPLE! BE SEATED!" said Alo, giving the public a moment to settle before continuing. "As we prepare for the BIGGEST rankings in our history, I ask that we take a moment to remember the strength of unity that this realm was built on. Remember that we are stronger when we stand on that unity and weaker when we are divided."

After a warm round of applause from most of the stadium, Alo continued, "I want to also give thanks to the ancestors, for without them, we would not be here, and the supreme Gods that watch over us, Shango, Yemaya, Gaia, and even Apophis ...."

The crowd erupted in laughter, and Alo's words ignited another wave of cheers that echoed around the stadium.

"This class is special to me as my own sons make their debut into the history books. I'm extremely proud, not only for them surviving the training isles but also for making it here on time. Thank you, Ganyah."

Amidst the laughter, boos erupted from the Zion section once again, and Cairo couldn't contain his rising anger at the disrespect shown to his father. Nevertheless, King Alo continued his speech with grace.

"I also want to honor my beloved Queen, who tirelessly worked day and night to bring this festival to life. So, rise to your feet, and let's warmly welcome the glue that holds our realm and my household together—the great, amazing Queen of Queens... NEBI AMAAN!"

The crowd erupted in cheers, and the Mansa section stomped their feet so vigorously that Cairo worried the floors might give way. As his mother descended to the podium, she expressed her gratitude to her husband and the realm before thanking the guardians for their assistance in preparing the cadets for the quest.

Suddenly, the lights darkened, and the focus was locked on the stage, setting the table for Nebi to invite the cadets down to receive their rankings.

"Now, without further ado... IT IS TIME TO ANNOUNCE THE TOP-RANKED CADETS! WHICH VILLAGE WILL CLAIM THE CHAMPIONSHIP THIS YEAR?!" Nebi declared, igniting the thousands of Umoyans.

"We take great pride in the integrity of our rankings. I can assure you that all votes were based solely on the cadet's performance during training. The village with the lowest average ranking score will take home the trophy. Good luck to all the villages. Good luck to all cadets and thank you for continuing a tradition set forth by our creators. Now, without further ado, let us begin!"

Tension skyrocketed as the stadium fell to a hush to hear every name Nebi announced. As she began calling each of the names, Cairo spotted Donovan and Maaku sneaking away from their table, out of his peripheral vision, and slipping into the stadium halls after speaking with a few guards standing watch at the Zion entrance. He signaled to Kane, who had noticed the same and raised his eyebrows questioningly. Kane nodded back, and they quietly slipped away from the table as the others remained engrossed in Queen Nebi's words.

"Kane and I will be right back," Cairo whispered to the table.

"And where are you two going?" Mariella asked.

"I'm coming! Tonight is not the night for one of your little stunts. Your mother is about to start the rankings," Serenity added.

"We will be right back. It's a hundred of us. I know for a fact neither of us will be called anytime soon," Cairo replied as he and Kane made their way toward the side entrance.

They headed into the stadium's halls, quietly hoping to catch up to Donovan and Maaku. They quickly found the sound of their voice, slowing down near a passage leading to a staircase.

"Slow down. If we go into the staircase now, they'll know we're following them," Kane suggested.

"That's fine; I'm not trying to sneak them or anything like that, although they would probably do that to us."

"Cairo, what are you talking about? I mean, follow them to find out where they're sneaking off to. Why did you think we came out here?" Kane asked, shaking his head in disappointment.

"I thought we were going to catch them and beat them down for what they pulled at Mars's truck," Cairo innocently claimed.

Kane gave him a skeptical look. "Sometimes you scare me, bro. No, we need to follow them. Figure out what they're up to. I get bad vibes every time I see them together."

Cairo sucked his teeth in frustration. "Oh, I thought we were about to press them. They could just be going to the bathroom. Can we at least approach them since we're already out here?"

"No, we cannot fight before getting on stage in front of the whole realm. I'm just trying to figure out what they're up to. Something about them doesn't sit right with me."

Kane led the way; Cairo followed behind closely to the staircase. Cairo stayed close by his brother as the door opened, and they could both hear Maaku and Donovan trying to whisper.

"I'm not going to keep blindly doing what Mara and Azazel tell me. Once my parents become the king and queen of Mansa, I will rule things differently." Maaku said in a smug tone.

"Maaku have faith in the process. My parents have their way, but I promise it'll make sure we all come out on top. Look how we took Zion." Donovan reassured.

"Yeah, I hear you. How much longer do we have to wait here?"

"Until we get the signal from Julara. She said that they're already putting everything into play now. Once she gets here, you just stay on the lookout by the bathroom. We'll handle everything else from there." Donovan answered.

"Well, they need to hurry up; I can hear Nebi already started going through the rankings. We need to be there when she calls our names."

"Calm down, we won't be here much longer. We have Zealots scattered throughout the stadium; they better get these rankings right."

"Yeah, they're pissing everyone off. I'd love to see the look on the council's face if we turned this place upside down."

"I know, right!"

"But don't you think if we cause a scene here, we should cancel the meet-up in the forest?"

"Nah, we'll be fine; they'll be too caught up in the festivities to pay us any mind. Nobody will even see us coming."

Cairo felt his blood boil as he heard the conversation between Donovan and Maaku unfold. Just as he was about to react, the two received an alert and quickly left the staircase, disappearing into the hall. Cairo looked at Kane, who was already on his way up the stairs.

Cairo quickly followed behind and spotted Donovan approaching the control rooms, leaving Maaku to stand guard near the end of the hall. A purple portal appeared after a quick incantation and quick hand gestures, and three hooded figures sporting silver demonic-faced masks emerged. Two of them were carrying a black body-sized bag. Kane and Cairo exchanged shocked glances before focusing back on the scene. The bag was leaking blood as they moved it to a nearby door.

Donovan followed behind the hooded figures into the control room. After a moment, Maaku stood in the middle of the hallway, idly waiting for the others to finish.

"We need to see what they're doing in that room," Kane whispered.

"I have a plan. Follow my lead and move on my signal."

Before Kane could ask about the details, Cairo opened the door. Maaku started speaking, and Cairo wasted no time, punching Maaku in the face with full force, immediately knocking him unconscious. Cairo signaled for Kane to come over.

"We can't see anything from the window; we have to go inside," Cairo said as Kane approached.

The brothers entered the hall leading to the power source room. As they approached, they noticed a trail of blood leading to the room at the end of the hall. The closer they got; Cairo could see the hooded figures dumping bodies out of the body bags.

Kane moved closer, but Cairo could hear Maaku groaning and starting to wake up. Cairo quickly tapped Kane and signaled it was time to go. They returned to the hall and kicked Maaku in the face, knocking him back out. The brothers then hurried back down the stairs and into the hallway.

As they returned to their table, Kane suddenly revealed, "Cairo, one of those dead bodies was Celeste."

Cairo was shocked. "Wait, are you sure?"

"Had to be. It was quick, but I know what I saw."

"What do we do?" Cairo asked.

"We have to say something!' Kane whispered frantically.

Cairo felt his heart drop as Kane's words sank in. The brothers hurried back to their section after hearing the staircase door open. They went through the halls back to their table, where their mother was still going through the rankings. Cairo did his best to maintain a poker face, even though his mind was plagued with thoughts of what could happen.

"Where the hell have you two been? You missed half the rankings; we're already down to the top ten," Vadé asked.

"Your mother has been flying through them since the people in Zion keep acting a damn fool," Mariella added, annoyed.

"Are you two, okay?" Serenity asked, eyeing Kane and Cairo closely.

"It's all a front. Where are the guards," Kane replied quickly.

"Wait, bro, look," Cairo mentioned, watching a set of guard's retreat into the same stadium hallway they just exited, passing Maaku and Donovan to their seats. Maaku shot Cairo a dirty look as he caressed his jaw that Cairo waved off unphased.

Cairo felt Serenity's eyes on him and tried to ignore it. His mind filled with thoughts of what he had witnessed. As the rankings continued, he couldn't shake off the unsettling feeling.

"And then there were five," Nebi announced with a twinkle in her eye. The spotlight beamed down on Cairo's table and Maaku's as the last of the cadets. Cairo did his best to conceal his nerves, not wanting the entire realm to see his anxiety.

"The fifth-ranked cadet is..." Nebi paused, enjoying the suspense. She glanced down at the name card, her lips curving into a mysterious smile before continuing, "Maaku LeReaux!" The cheers erupted, although they dwindled as the audience witnessed Maaku's distraught expression. Kane and Cairo sat frozen, eyeing him with contempt as he approached the stage. Nebi waited for Maaku to find his place in formation before addressing the arena again.

"Our fourth-ranked trainee will be...." Nebi paused, causing Cairo's anxiety to skyrocket as he was sure she was about to say his name.

"SERENITY TESSAY FROM ZION!" Nebi announced loudly. The Zion fan section erupted with cheers and songs as silver rockets filled the air in celebration of Zion's second highest-ranked cadet.

Serenity rose from her seat at the table as if caught in a waking dream. As she stood, Cairo enveloped her in a distracted embrace, casting wary glances down the dimly lit hallway.

"You've worked so hard for this very moment! I'm proud of you!" Kane whispered gently into her ear.

"Thank you, Kane," she replied, managing a grateful smile while suppressing tears that threatened to spill.

Determined, she ventured toward the grand stadium, where the Queen and council members greeted her with applause. Serenity assumed her place among the elite cadets, eagerly awaiting the next turn of events. On the jumbotron, images of Donovan, Cairo, and Kane appeared, their anxious faces displayed for the entire stadium.

"Only three cadets remain, with two hailing from the village of Mansa and one representing the resilient village of Zion. Will the final three contestants kindly make their way to the stage?" Queen Nebi's voice echoed through the stadium; her arms raised triumphantly. The tension between Zion and Mansa was palpable, for Donovan's rank could send Zion its first championship in village history.

Kane led Cairo as they ascended the stage, ignoring the boos from the Zion crowd. Memories of bloodstained halls and fallen comrades haunted Cairo as Donovan met them on stage, waiting for their fate to be sealed.

"Please step onto the central platforms," Nebi instructed, guiding the three young men. "These platforms will ascend, with the highest-ranking cadet securing the coveted number one spot."

Cairo stepped onto the platform with Kane and Donovan beside him. Gazing into the crowd, Cairo felt a profound sense of purpose over him. He closed his eyes as the platform elevated, his heart sinking as it eventually halted. The crowd's frenzy reached its zenith as he opened his eyes.

"Ladies and gentlemen, our top-ranked cadets are DONOVANN HEWALE at number three, KANE AMAAN at number two, and the distinguished title of the number one ranked cadet in Umoyan history goes to none other than CAIRO AMAN!" Nebi's voice resonated with pride, and Cairo exulted, arms raised high. Kane smiled at him while Donovan's visage twisted with disdain. Ignoring them, Cairo basked in triumph until he glimpsed the crowd.

A significant section of Zion had turned their backs on him, expressing their disdain openly. Cairo's blood boiled as many of them began making their way out of the stadium.

As the platforms descended back to the stage, darkness shrouded the entire stadium, inciting confusion and a few startled screams. Cairo's head spun in bewilderment, spotting Manny rushing to Alo and Nebi's side before she wielded her staff. Alo, stepping down from his throne, thrust his hands to the sky, attempting to conjure light, but it quickly flickered and dimmed. His efforts forced him to a knee, causing a commotion. Guards came to his aid as Nebi raised her staff, the crystal atop radiating a soothing glow, silencing the crowd. Nebi lifted the luminous staff to her lips, using it as an impromptu microphone.

"Please, stay calm! We've experienced a temporary power outage due to system overload. We'll continue the celebration in the court-yards outside the capital. Please follow the ushers' guidance to find the nearest exit."

Cairo felt someone tugging at his arm and turned to see Manny guiding him and Kane to the stage's side.

"Come quickly, my princes. We must get out of here at once."

"What in the world is happening, Manny?" Cairo inquired, already expecting him to tell him about the bodies they found.

"Once we reach a more secure location, I'll explain everything," Manny insisted.

CHAPTER 7
BEWARE
SERENITY

As the illuminated lights permeated the arena once more, the cadets were quickly separated by village and guided back to their respective sections. Accompanied by her fellow cadets, Serenity followed the security detail to a chamber deep within the stadium, where they awaited further developments.

As she entered, an awkward wave of uncertainty rippled through her peers. The investigation into the power outage and the sudden protest had left little room for genuine engagement. Soon, Azazel and Mara entered, their presence commanding an immediate hush in the divided room, their faces mirroring a sense of discomfort as if they'd rather be anywhere else in the world.

"We were robbed," Mara stated angrily, her voice filled with emotion. "We will not continue to be disrespected."

"I believe what the Queen is saying," Azazel interjected, glancing nervously at his wife. "We are disappointed. As a village, we were not unified, and during times like these, we must stand together. If one protests the results, we need to be united."

Serenity felt Mara's gaze lock onto her for a brief, piercing moment as if burning into the side of her face from across the room.

"I am proud of those who chose to stand against the constant disrespect," Mara added, still staring in Serenity's direction.

A weak and anxious applause circled the room before Azazel raised his hand for silence.

"We seem to have caused quite the stir after the recent events. Therefore, we are mandating that every Zion cadet ride back with us to the village. We will meet at the stadium's south entrance within the next fifteen minutes."

"Transportation will depart shortly after," Mara added with a veiled threat as she motioned for the door, "If you get left behind, you'll have to find your own way back to the village."

Once the door closed behind them, a few guards stood staring blank-faced at the room's corners.

"Girl, the tea is hot!" Missy whispered from behind Serenity. "Even I didn't know about the protest. We are definitely about to go to war now."

"Missy, calm down," Serenity commanded. "Ain't nobody going to war."

"Did you see what I saw before the lights went out? It was almost a riot! Thank the Gods, Nebi did what she did."

Serenity glanced at her watch, only to find it unresponsive. She tried to adjust the device's settings to no avail before swiping the screen away in frustration.

"Interference," another Zion cadet interjected. "Nobody can call or get in touch with us down here. They've got us locked up like animals."

"Well, if some of y'all didn't jump up and ruin the festival, we wouldn't be down here. I can't believe they've got me caught up in y'all mess." Missy fired off.

"You didn't see me standing up!! I didn't want to be associated with that! We were also being celebrated, but that got ruined because we lost the championship," said another voice.

"Yeah, at least we got second this year," came another voice.

"Y'all sound weak," Donovan barked, parting with the few Zion cadets near Serenity. "You should be tired of them looking down on us. This is bigger than the festival, and it's scary that you don't even see that."

"Here you go," said Missy, sucking her teeth.

"The day will come when you will have to make a choice. If you don't make it, those other villages will," Donovan continued.

Serenity watched as his words swayed a few Zion cadets, many of whom had protested with him. The sentiment spread throughout the room, infecting most cadets and making her feel almost surrounded by his influence.

"There's a right and a wrong way to do things," Serenity said, finding her voice among the chatter.

"Yeah, and how they treat us is wrong!" Donovan fired back.

"Speak for yourself. I spend a lot of time in the other villages, and I've never been treated any differently," Serenity argued.

"They just cheated us! You've always made excuses for them because you're the princess's sidekick. The rest of us get treated as second-class citizens."

"That's right!" a voice cried out in support of the Zion prince.

"Not to mention, you're all wrapped up with the jaded prince. You need to drop him and deal with someone worth your time," Donovan taunted, offering a wink.

"I'm nobody's sidekick, unlike you; you became the prince of Zion only to follow behind Maaku? Make it make sense, Donny boy! How are you worth my time when I almost outranked you? I promise you; nobody thinks of you as much as you think."

Serenity's response elicited laughter from Missy, which rippled around the room, and even Donovan, doing his best to hide his embarrassment, joined in with a feigned laugh.

"You think you're funny?" Donovan retorted.

"She is," Missy chimed in between her chuckles.

Donovan leaned in by Serenity's ear. "You better get on the right side of history before it's too late."

Before Serenity could utter another retort, the room's doors flung open, silencing everyone. A Zion guard appeared, clutching an energy weapon tightly. He gestured silently for the cadets to follow him, and they complied, falling into line and tiptoeing behind him and the guards.

Serenity allowed everyone to go ahead of her before slipping quietly into a side room filled with spare chairs and tables. She waited a few moments and peeked into the empty hallway, contemplating finding her way out of the stadium.

Just as she was mustering the nerve to exit, Nebi, accompanied by Ganyah and a few men she didn't recognize, rushed past the door in a fury. She came to a sudden halt a few feet down the hallway and issued orders to secure the hall. She commanded Ganyah to make his post here while she figured out the details of the blackout.

Nebi took off down the hallway, and for a second, Ganyah turned his attention to the partially open door. Fearing that closing it would attract even more attention, Serenity left it slightly ajar, held her breath, and slowly backed away.

She nearly jumped out of her skin when the door suddenly flung open, and Ganyah, her trainer, stood there, gazing at her as if he had known Serenity was there the entire time.

"What are you doing?" he inquired with a light-hearted tone.

"I... I didn't want to—"

"It's okay. Don't worry about it. Get yourself together," Ganyah reassured, closing the door behind him.

"You'll have to get to Queen Iris and Osanyin."

"Okay," Serenity agreed, unable to find it within her to object.

"Ranked fourth for a cadet that everyone had ranked forty-ninth in the pre-rankings is pretty impressive. You did good, kid. You did good."

Serenity couldn't hide her smile as she started. "Thank you so much for choosing me to train with the princes. You could have selected any other trainee in the class, but you chose me. I'll never understand it, but thank you for believing in me, Ganyah,"

Ganyah stepped back and knelt before her, ensuring she could witness the sincerity in his eyes. "I told you before—I chose you because I saw something in you that I've never seen in anyone else, not even in our princes. They need you more than you'll ever understand," Ganyah declared, his tone resolute.

Ganyah retrieved a necklace adorned with glistening diamonds from the inner pocket of his suit jacket. The precious stones shimmered under the gallery lighting as they dangled from his fingers. Serenity's eyes filled with silent tears as she examined the exquisite necklace. In a surge of emotion, she jumped up and wrapped her arms around Ganyah's neck.

"Thank you, thank you, thank you! Thank you for everything, Ganyah. Thank you for taking a chance on me!"

The sound of approaching footsteps filled the hallways, pulling them away from their precious moment. Ganyah gripped Serenity's hand and led her out of the room, meeting the guards accompanying an exhausted King. Alo seemed relieved to see his good friend as Ganyah helped him shuffle down the hallway.

"We have to get to the mansion," Alo whispered.

"I know. I got ya," Ganyah insisted. "You two make sure transportation is ready. The Queen has instructed me to go ahead without her."

"Where... where is... Nebi?" Alo asked, using the last of his strength to look around for his Queen.

"She will meet you at the mansion. Come on," Ganyah urged. "The girl is with me. See that she is taken to Osanyin and Queen Iris immediately."

"Indeed," boomed one of the colossal soldiers, his voice resonating like the echoes of an ancient incantation.

"Find Mariella and stay with her. I will find you later," Ganyah declared, his regal presence unwavering as he delicately supported the ailing King, Alo, wrapping the monarch's arm around his neck.

Serenity nodded solemnly; her words lost in the depths of her empathy for the legendary King. She fell into step behind the Mansa guards, who moved with an urgency that threatened to force her into a brisk jog to keep pace.

They were almost at the stairway when they discovered Queen Nebi backing out of the control room, her face a portrait of horror. The Mansa guards rushed to her defense as dozens of wily badger rats scurried from the room. Serenity deftly leaped out of their path and inched closer, her curiosity piqued by the Queen's fearful gaze within the control room.

Nebi snapped out of her horrified trance and promptly closed the doors, finally acknowledging Serenity's presence. "Get her out of here immediately," she ordered without a direct glance, and the guards hustled Serenity away, leading her up the stairs and out of the stadium through the back exit.

The front of the stadium was already crowded with irate Umoyans demanding answers about the abrupt end to the festival, some chanting "Down with Zion ". At the same time, more guards converged to maintain order.

Amid the chaos, the Zone G cadets had gathered near the transportation docks. Serenity's heart quickened as she spotted Mariella laughing with her fellow cadets at the forefront. Mariella's joviality faded as she noticed Serenity's disconcerted expression and rushed forward to embrace her friend.

"What's wrong?" Mariella inquired, her concern evident. "Why you look like you just saw Kane with another girl?"

Serenity waited until the guards retreated into the stadium before confiding, "I think something bad is happening. I saw the Queen on the way out, and she saw something in a room filled with rats that spooked her."

"Spooked her?" Mariella questioned.

"Yeah," Serenity confirmed. "She shut the door to keep me from seeing, but whatever was inside bothered her."

"It couldn't have been badger rats that caused the stadium shutdown," Mariella mused, a grimace of distaste on her face.

Serenity added, "Rats were there, but she didn't even react to them. She was fixated on something deeper in that room."

"I wonder what it could be," Mariella pondered briefly before shrugging. "Is the rest of Zion returning to the village?"

Serenity nodded with a hint of apprehension. "No one had much of a choice. I had to slip away."

"Figures! My father has already arranged transportation for me, but given this chaos, I doubt they'll arrive anytime soon."

"Well," Serenity shrugged, a sense of foreboding casting its shadow. "Something tells me things are about to get even crazier."

Serenity's sharp eyes caught sight of Mars conversing with a group of agitated rioters at the back of the tumultuous crowd. Overwhelmed by the news he had received; he bore an expression of profound grief. "Is that Mars?" she wondered aloud.

Mariella squinted and spotted him swiftly making his way through the restless crowd, heading back toward the vendor square. Serenity and Mariella swiftly followed him, weaving through a sea of festive Umoyans. The peculiar mix of celebrating and seeking confrontation after the Zion fiasco created a surreal and tense atmosphere.

They reached Mars's truck, and he slammed the door shut behind him, unaware he was being followed. Serenity and Mariella exchanged puzzled glances and peered through one of the windows. Inside, Mars sat in the back, tears streaming down his face as he smoked a joint and listened to music on his headphones. Mariella tapped on the window, but Mars remained lost in his own world, seemingly unaware of their presence.

"Give me a moment," Mariella insisted.

"Of course, I'll be right here," Serenity assured her.

As Mariella made her way to the back of Mars's truck, Serenity observed the multitude of guards attempting to restore order in the chaotic scene. Shareeva, on the other hand, moved freely through the streets, her stern expression a potent weapon in itself.

It wasn't long before Shareeva noticed Serenity and started

heading toward her. Realizing that Shareeva's presence could further agitate Mars, Serenity swiftly disappeared into the bustling crowd, hoping to shake off anyone following her. In her haste, she accidentally collided with a hurried passerby. Annoyed, she turned to see who had nearly knocked her to the ground, only to be met with a feeling of disgust. It was Maaku who offered a disdainful scoff before rushing off toward the outskirts of the city.

She finally sought refuge at a nearby jewelry vendor's stall, hoping to avoid more encounters. The vendor greeted her with a smile, but it vanished as Shareeva's frail hand landed on Serenity's shoulder.

"Well, well, well, look at the spectacle here," Shareeva observed, taking in the chaotic scene. "The age of Apophis has started with a bang!"

"What do you want?" Serenity replied, her voice laced with defiance.

The vendor chose to retreat into his tent, refusing to get involved with the notorious witch.

"It's quite sad that you don't realize how much I could do for you, more than you can imagine," Shareeva offered.

"Tell me, Shareeva, what do you think you could do for me?" Serenity asked.

"Is your mother still ill?" Shareeva inquired, taking a drag from her purple cigar.

"Who told you about my mother?" Serenity's face filled with concern.

"I've been here longer than you can imagine. There's not much happening that I don't know about. Besides, I'm here to tell you I could teach you how to heal her. You could bypass this perilous path to greatness and learn to harness the true magic of Apophis's gift to Umoya."

"Xenyd," Serenity muttered in a grim tone.

"That's right," Shareeva replied with a toothy grin. "Out with the old, in with the new era, where the last shall be first. You're quite familiar with that concept, aren't you?"

Shareeva's words struck a chord deep within Serenity as memories of Ganyah assisting King Alo flashed before her eyes. Her gaze shifted, clouded with emotions, and Shareeva, with her twisted smile, didn't miss the change.

"Are you alright? You look like you've seen a ghost," Shareeva remarked with a hint of mockery.

"Shareeva, I don't need you or your dust, which seems to bring you closer to death every day, to care for my mother. The gods will show me the way."

"And which of the sacred gods do you think will reveal themselves to you, little Miss Zion?"

"I'm not sure, and I'm alright with that," Serenity said, finding her confidence.

"Oh, I'm sure you are. With your family's history, do you think it's a coincidence that you seem to be thriving in these times, or could it be because you have the blood of Apophis running through your veins?"

Serenity's anger flared, "What are you talking about?" she snapped. "Stop acting like you know anything about me or my family!"

"As usual, you have no clue what you're talking about," Shareeva retorted. "But that will change. You won't have a choice soon. I have answers to questions you didn't even know you had. If you were smart, you'd join me and claim everything you've ever desired."

"You don't even have everything you want. How can you give me what you don't have?" Serenity questioned.

"The age of Apophis is here. Understand that your parents knew what you would become. With your potential and your mother's precious bloodline, you could be one of the strongest Umoyans in the realm. Follow the right path."

"You know nothing about my father, and you clearly don't know anything about my mother! I am where I am because of the gods. I don't need you, your dust, or your magic. I'll follow the path of tradition," Serenity retorted, her resolve strengthening as she noticed Mariella searching for her.

"Sweet child, you have so much to learn, and your loyalty is blind. When you're ready, I'll be here just like I've always been for your family. You can deny fate only for so long. Until next time, Little Miss Zion."

As Serenity made her way to a concerned Mariella, Shareeva's cryptic offer and insights into Serenity's family weighed heavily in the air, leaving Serenity grappling with a whirlwind of emotions and uncertainties.

CHAPTER 8
STANDING ON BUSINESS
NEBI

The mayhem in the stadium had finally subsided, leaving Nebi to grapple with the echoes of chaos within her. Determined, she embarked on a journey to Zion, her heart heavy with the responsibility of confronting Mara and Azazel. Seated in the back of a sleek, black hover car, staff tightly gripped in her hand, Nebi's composed exterior betrayed none of the turmoil churning within.

The hovercar glided to a halt before a grand black mansion, an imposing structure mirroring Nebi's authority. A message from Ark reassured her of Kane and Cairo's safety, momentarily lifting the burden from her shoulders.

The private neighborhood in Zion exuded an eerie ambiance, with homes draped in dreary black and gray hues. Mara and Azazel's mansion loomed at the end of a secluded street; an enigma veiled in haunting mystery.

Nebi emerged from the hover car, commanding the driver to stop, her posture resolute. Three more vehicles, filled with security personnel, lined up behind her, ready to follow her lead. She instructed them to remain vigilant from a distance as she approached the mansion's entrance.

A solid gray door swung open, revealing Azazel. Nebi entered with determination, the opulent marble floors beneath her feet contrasting starkly with the oppressive atmosphere. The scent of an attic hung in the air, and despite the luxury, the mansion felt like a gilded prison. The chandelier bathed the space in harsh light, accentuating the dreariness of the color scheme.

Nebi's piercing gaze locked onto Azazel as she demanded, "Where is Mara?" A silent intensity burned in her eyes, delving into his very soul.

With caution, Azazel responded, "She is upstairs. She will be down in a second. I can't say this visit is unexpected."

Nebi's voice held unwavering determination, "You and Mara will have to stand before the Royal Council for what you've done. I will not allow you to divide our realm!"

Mara's smooth and commanding voice interrupted from the top of a grand staircase, "Allow Nebi and me to speak one-on-one." She descended in a shimmering silver robe, and with a smug demeanor, Azazel excused himself to attend to security details.

Alone, Mara gestured toward a black couch, offering hospitality Nebi rejected with a flare of her nose. The air thickened with tension as the two influential figures confronted each other.

"You look rather upset by the protest, but I don't think that's why you're here, is it?" Mara began.

"Elise Mekari, Celeste Folora, Neru Hin, and Beraldi Creed. Those are the names of the people your people murdered tonight," Nebi's eyes blazed with an intensity matching the fire within her.

"Murdered? You said Celeste wasn't on stage at the rankings because she was sick. Now you're telling me she's dead?"

"Mara, I found the bodies and the badger rats you left behind. There's no need for you to play games with me." Nebi's nostrils flared, and her gaze remained unrelenting.

Mara's response shifted, her surprise evident. "Accusing me of murder in my own home? You're misguided, Queen. I'm no genius, but if it's badger rats you found, shouldn't you be knocking on Iris's door? Badger rats are only native in Zone G last I checked," she retorted smugly.

Nebi's gaze remained unwavering, "Well, right now, I'm talking to you. You made your point tonight. Now it's time to stand on it," she declared, tightening her grip on her staff as the maisha stone adorned at the top began to cast a pure white light.

"Nebi, listen to me. We've had our moments. I revel in taking you on verbally in meetings, but I would never stoop to murder. Our protest was our message; anything else wasn't us. Talk to me. What did you find?"

Before Nebi could respond, Azazel rushed into the room with a worried look. Nebi and Mara rose to their feet, anticipation hanging in the air. Azazel quickly shut the door, locking it and extinguishing the lights.

"What is going on, Azazel?" Nebi demanded.

"I'm not sure. Our security told me to run in here with you and shut off the lights immediately. They didn't say what the—" Azazel's words hung in the air, a tense silence enveloping the room.

The air in the room turned thick with dread as a crystallized bullet abruptly ended Azazel's life. Nebi, horror etched across her face, watched him fall. As Mara cradled Azazel, Nebi's shock dissolved into action. Pointing her staff at Azazel, a white light began to form, ready to invoke the powers within her. However, another crystallized bullet pierced through the window.

Nebi's white light absorbed the bullet, leaving a small metal fragment on the ground. Pocketing the metal piece, she moved to the window, witnessing chaos outside as her security scrambled to find the assailant. Mara's tearful plea for justice echoed in the background as Nebi vowed to uncover the truth.

Feeling the weight of Azazel's death, Nebi took a deep breath, allowing her goddess form to take hold. Outside, she raised her staff to the moon, the celestial light scanning the area, revealing the auras of all living organisms. Unable to find the assailant, she returned to normal as Manny approached.

Manny urgently led Nebi to the hover car, instructing the guards to stay with Mara. As they sped away, Nebi pressed Manny for details. Manny revealed the surprise attack by three individuals who vanished in purple smoke, leaving no trace. Nebi's mind raced with the implications.

Replaying the event, Nebi examined the metal fragment, her lunar energy rendering it unrecognizable. As her anxiety eased, she answered Shunny's urgent call, only to be met with the news of Hiram being attacked by Zion. Shunny's voice thundered through the line, declaring war.

Nebi, trying to steady herself, questioned the details, "What do you mean war? What happened?" Nebi's voice quickened with concern.

"Not only did they ruin our son's cherished moment at the festival, but Safan just fought off four zealots trying to ambush us here in our home."

"I don't think Zion is behind this; They were just attacked right before my eyes! Azazel is dead!"

"What in the name of the supreme Gods is happening?" Shunny thundered.

"If dark magic is at play, we need to find Shareeva. She's our best shot to help us figure out what's happening."

"You're right! She's the one who warned me of the attack," Shunny said with genuine curiosity.

"You, see? Did you ask her how she knew?" Nebi retorted.

"She claimed to have overheard murmurs among the protestors outside the stadium. She's in route to your palace to check on the boys. I contacted you the moment we were safe."

"I'll contact her, but Shunny, someone has killed the king of Zion and targeted Mara. Manny saw the assailants vanishing in purple smoke, and I found a bullet made of Xenyd. We may already be plunging into war."

"Azazel is gone?" Shunny asked somberly, finally realizing the gravity of Nebi's words.

"Yes!" Nebi replied with icy composure. "We must safeguard our realm, Shunny. I'm in route to Iris's to follow up on something. Keep your security detail on high alert."

"What about Mara? If Azazel is gone, is she safe?" Shunny's voice softened with concern.

"She will be secure; my security detail is with her. I cannot vouch for the turmoil in her mind right now. When I get more info, I will call you back. I love you, Shunny. Be safe."

"I love you too," Shunny responded the connection lingering with a blend of worry and determination.

Ending the call with her sister, Nebi guided the hover car through the rural streets of Zone G. She contemplated reaching out to Shareeva, but Manny's mention of the ominous purple smoke gave her pause. *Something doesn't feel right,* she thought to herself.

Azazel's demise dealt a blow to Nebi's pride, leaving her powerless. Despite wielding the limitless power of the moon, she stood there, unable to save him. With her children on the brink of embarking on the quest, her heart bore the weight of the impending challenges. However, Nebi knew now was not the time to succumb to the weight of emotions; it was time to stand resolute under the looming pressure.

The journey proved brief; they reached the lush Zone G palace, its country charm accentuated by acres of sprawling land. Animals of every kind greeted Nebi as she approached the entrance, acknowledging her presence with a sense of reverence. Upon ringing the doorbell of the imposing black wood door, Nebi was met by Iris, adorned with her distinctive blue curly hair, green fur, shades, a silk robe, and a green joint hanging casually from her lips.

Iris ushered Nebi into her chaotic yet elegant abode, where the natural scent of incense enveloped Nebi as she navigated through the whirlwind of Iris's palace. The walls, each adorned in a different color, reflected Iris's indecisiveness. At the same time, white marble floors bore the imprints of various animal footprints, aside from the occasional ash on the ground.

Despite the unconventional surroundings, Iris usually maintained a reasonably tidy home. This time, however, things looked as if a toddler had a fit in every room of the house.

"You're here about the Zealots, aren't you?" Iris questioned, taking a long drag from her joint, "I'm afraid you won't find them useful. They've already been dealt with; my animal hive is having their dinner as we speak."

"What! The Zealots were already here? Did you get any information from them before you fed them to your...friends?" Nebi looked at her friend, eyes wide with shock.

"I didn't need to," Iris said, sipping her drink.

"What do you mean? What was it? Who is behind these attacks?" Nebi asked.

"Nebi, you're my best friend, right?" Iris asked in an innocent but guilty tone.

"Of course, blood couldn't make us any closer," Nebi responded, slightly confused.

"Okay, so I'm going to say a lot, and I need you just to listen before you respond," Iris requested, finishing her cup.

"Ok," Nebi said through squinted eyes, holding her staff close, her Maisha stone glowing white at the ready.

"So, while the kids were away at the training isles..." Iris paused, taking a last gulp of her drink and putting out her joint. "While the kids were away at the training isles, Shareeva approached me one day."

"I don't understand," Nebi said, following along.

"She came to me and asked for access to the forests of Zone G. I told her she would have to kill me before I let her have access to the type of magic Zone G forests hold. She told me if I didn't give it to her, she would tell Osanyin..." Iris kept the dramatics going, pausing and taking a deep breath.

"Tell Osanyin what?" Nebi asked, trying to read Iris's face.

"About Ganyah," Iris said, staring at Nebi, hoping she wouldn't make her elaborate.

Nebi stared at her friend for a moment in disbelief, almost unable to process the words that her lips spewed before she finally found her voice, "So are you saying Shareeva is behind this? Azazel is dead, and if this is Shareeva, you put us all in danger," Nebi said, her voice tinged with anger.

"Nebi, my children are my world. I couldn't imagine Mars and Mariella finding out the truth like that, especially from her. I never wanted to do it, but what other option did I have?" Iris said, eyes closed.

"YOU COULD'VE TOLD THE TRUTH!" Nebi growled, standing up. "I told you back then that asking for Shareeva's help with your lies was a bad idea! Now she has access to the magic of Zone G's Forest, and she sent her goons to take us out!" Nebi said, feeling her blood boil.

"I wanted to tell the truth, but then after Mars saw Shareeva in the woods, everything just happened so fast."

Nebi's eyes widened as she recognized a truth, she had been blind to. "Wait a minute. Did Mars see Shareeva in the forest? Is that what he told you?"

"I.... I"

"Iris!" Nebi shrieked, unable to sit any longer, "You had my nephew living out of a trailer and painted him as some drugged fanatic for the entire realm, AND THAT ENTIRE TIME YOU WAS LYING!!"

"I had to figure out what to do, Nebi! I don't want my family to fall apart!"

"Oh, so the realm can fall apart so long as your family stays intact, huh?"

"Please try to understand, I was only —"

"Cut the excuses, Iris. No matter how you try to spin it, all this falls in your lap! What did Mars see Shareeva doing in the forest?"

"Nebi, you have to understand," Iris pleaded.

"What did he say!?"

"She was after the blood of the black unicorn. He saw her performing some sort of ritual."

Nebi's heart nearly stopped as the words hit her in her soul, for she knew that using unicorn blood meant that she was attempting to amplify her ability to wield dark magic.

"I think she's using Xenyd again, Nebi. She may have even found a way to resurrect the Ighandi. Mars said he saw a hissing creature reach out of the flames and grab a unicorn into a portal with one arm."

Iris's words faded into nothingness as Nebi's mind raced. Her thoughts felt so loud it was a wonder that Iris couldn't hear them. Her body suddenly felt numb as all the pieces to the puzzle plaguing the realm were finally beginning to show a clearer picture.

"Are you...ok Nebi?"

"No, I'm not ok," she said, fighting to keep her composure. "You're telling me my sister is using forbidden dark magic, maybe even resurrected the species that nearly ended the realm already. My friend has been lying to me for months, and the only person I can trust is —" Nebi paused momentarily, trying to force back her emotions.

"Nebi, I'm sorry."

"If she's found a way to gain enough power to resurrect the Ighandi, then she's probably the one behind all this mess. You were attacked! Azazel is dead!"

"Was Shunny attacked? Is she ok?

"Safan fought off four zealots trying to ambush them in their home. She said Shareeva —"

"Shareeva, what?" Iris asked.

"She said Shareeva warned her."

"So, if she's behind this, why would she warn Shunny? None of this is making sense."

The question sparked a thought in Nebi's head that made her freeze in her tracks. Frustrated, she quickly brought up a holographic call, and Manny promptly answered. Nebi didn't even give him a chance to greet her before she bombarded him with questions, "Is everything ok? Where is King Alo?"

He's resting in your chambers, Queen. He's stable but —"

"Where are the boys? Are they ok?"

"Last I checked, Ja'el was in his room sleeping while Kane and Cairo were in their room waiting to see if all the festivities were canceled. Ark and Shareeva are here helping me hold down the fort."

"I want more guards there now! We are under attack! Lock it down. Don't let Shareeva leave your sight. Do you understand!"

"Yes, Queen, is everything alright?"

"It will be when I get there."

Nebi swiped away the screen in frustration.

"What is going on?" Iris asked, confused.

"Shareeva is at my house right now! I need to go."

"What are you going to do?"

Nebi shook her head and shrugged her shoulders, unable to find the words to answer her question.

"How can I help?" Iris asked softly.

"You've done enough; your lies are why we are here now. The Iris, I know, would've never put us in this position in the first place!"

"You're right! I will make this right!"

Nebi scoffed sarcastically before coldly turning on her heels and heading for the door.

"I'm coming with you! There is no way I will let you deal with my mess alone!"

Iris reached for the door to follow Nebi out when Nebi swiped her arm away and pushed her away before she could interlock her fingers around the door. Frustrated, Iris tried again to make a motion out the door when Nebi suddenly smacked Iris with her glowing white staff as hard as she could. Iris flew across the room as Nebi swiftly moved to Iris, snatching her up. Nebi grabbed her by the throat and pushed her up against the wall.

Iris struggled against Nebi's grip. A white light began to

permeate around her hand, flashing around Iris's throat. Nebi looked into Iris's green eyes, remembering their bond, and let her go. Iris fell to the ground, coughing, trying to catch her breath as Nebi composed herself.

"Your sins will catch up with you, Iris. But until then, you will help clean up this mess you helped create. You will wait for my instructions to the letter. If you don't, I hope you recognize that you will be useless to me or the realm."

Iris looked up at Nebi as she fumed, her fear evident, "I...I understand."

Nebi shook her head with one long-lasting, tense look and headed out the door. She walked to her car with a face of stone until she finally found herself alone in the privacy of her backseat. She stared out the window as the vehicle zoomed in the direction of her home, and the tears flowed silently down her cheeks.

CHAPTER 9
FAMILY OVER EVERYTHING
CAIRO

Mom's going to be pissed," Kane muttered as he and Cairo stood in Cairo's aquamarine grand bedroom.

"Yeah, well, what choice do we have? You heard how Mariella sounded on the phone; we can't just sit in our rooms!"

Kane let out a deep sigh, accepting Cairo was right. "Where are they meeting us?"

"Through the back entrance of the palace. Mariella said they should be here any minute."

"You know security is not about to let them in,"

"That's why we're sneaking out; we meet them and head to the forest."

"I guess Cairo, it's not our worst plan ever. It's bad enough that Shareeva was here when she could be behind all this."

"Well, we won't find out anything sitting around here," Cairo answered.

"I hear you. Let's just go."

"Good, Ja'el will send us a message if they come looking for us. Let's head out before Ark checks in on us again."

Kane nodded, and the siblings headed out of their grand palace.

Maneuvering through their childhood grounds while avoiding prying eyes, it was clear they'd done this before. Eventually, they reached the far end gate and saw Serenity and Mariella standing waiting for them. They quickly met up and made their way out of sight of the palace's guards in the forest.

"Did you have any trouble getting here?" Kane asked the ladies.

"Not really," Serenity started.

"Is Mars coming?" Cairo asked.

"He left," Mariella replied curtly. "His Underground brothers and sisters came, and they went to conduct a ceremony for Ms. Mekari."

"Ceremony?" Cairo asked, puzzled.

"She is the founder of the underground. She was killed and dumped in the stadium," Mariella said, disgusted.

"And I think your mother is the one who found her," Serenity added.

Cairo locked eyes with Kane, and a wave of panic washed over him as the reality of Mariella's words sank in, chilling him to the core.

"What's wrong?" Serenity immediately inquired, sensing their distress.

"At the festival, when we left the table, we saw Donovan and Maaku helping the Zealots move their bodies," Kane said in a hushed tone. "Celeste was one of the bodies in the room with Ms. Mekari."

"Wait, what?" Serenity gasped. "Missy and her family have been looking for that girl all day!"

"I didn't see her; Kane had to tell me," Cairo explained.

"I didn't get a chance to see who the other bodies were before we had to get out of there," Kane added.

Mariella questioned, "So Maaku and Donovan are Zealots?"

"If they're helping them, they have to be," Cairo exclaimed, his anger simmering.

"Well, I just saw Maaku leaving Vendor Square not too long ago," Serenity informed them.

Cairo, irritated, asked, "What was he doing?"

"Nothing, he was by himself. It looked like he was rushing to head out of the city," Serenity replied.

"Wait," Kane exclaimed, his eyes lighting up with an idea. "Maaku said something about meeting in the woods. That's probably where he was headed."

"You're right," Cairo chimed in, the memory resurfacing. "They said they were meeting up later. He said his parents took control of Zion and to trust the process."

"We get to the woods, we find Maaku and the rest of the Zealots," Serenity suggested.

"And we get the answers we need even if we have to beat it out of them," Cairo added emphatically.

"I'm tired of playing defense. We need to figure out what's going on," Kane declared.

"Agreed," Serenity and Mariella said in unison.

The group pressed on, determined to make their way to the woods. The forest exuded an eerie stillness, and a mysterious mist hung over the waters, settling among the forest floor. The sun had already dipped below the towering amber trees, and their sap shimmered against the night sky, guiding their way.

They proceeded cautiously through the mist, searching for any sign of the Zealots. Still, the shroud of fog revealed nothing, only the familiar forest sounds—exotic creatures calling and crying out into the night skies.

"It feels like we've been walking in circles," Cairo finally exclaimed.

"Cairo's right, we need a plan. Wandering in the forest won't get us anywhere," Mariella agreed.

"What's the plan, bro?" Cairo asked, coming to a halt.

"They're out here," Kane insisted, his determination unwavering, "I can feel it."

"Here we go," Serenity said, chuckling to herself.

"What?" Mariella asked, perplexed.

"Just wait," Cairo advised. "This is what he does. You kind of have to go with it."

"I have to admit, he hasn't missed yet," Serenity added.

The group watched as Kane carefully surveyed his surroundings, examining the nearby trees and shrubs before finally pressing his palm to the ground. He closed his eyes for a moment, a smile gracing his face.

"Follow me," he declared, taking off into the mist.

"I told you," Cairo remarked, and he promptly followed his brother, with Serenity and Mariella close behind.

As Kane finally came to a halt on a bluff, he quickly turned around, motioning for everyone to stay quiet and get low. Crouching beside his brother, Cairo peered over the cliff and spotted a group of individuals dressed in black hoods and silver demonic masks gathered below.

Cairo motioned to jump down and attack, but Kane stopped him before he could reveal himself. "Just wait," he cautioned.

"Where are the others?" one of the voices cried out. Cairo couldn't discern the voice, as it seemed cloaked with technology.

"Relax, they will be here soon, and then we will carry out the plan. The King is weak; he dies tonight, and we will control another village," one of the masked figures declared.

Cairo gripped the dirt, his emotions broiling as he heard the sinister intentions of the Zealots unfolding. He shot a look of rage at his brother, urging him to signal the charge before he could no longer resist.

"When we go in there, our orders are to take out everyone. Remember, we only have a few minutes to get in and out. Leave nothing unturned, and nobody breathing! Long live Shakur!" one of the Zealots declared.

"Long live Shakur!" the Zealots chanted before reaching into a pocket within their hoodies and pulling out a small pouch. They each inhaled a purple dust that left them twitching for a moment before a burst of purple energy erupted from their feet, and their auras began to glow with a purple hue.

Unable to restrain himself any longer, Cairo leaped from the cliff, ripping the ring off his hand and summoning his staff. With all his strength, he drove it as hard as he could into the skull of one of the Zealots and then swept his leg to kick the Zealot so severely that the Zealot flew into a nearby tree.

Cairo quickly counted ten Zealots, all turning their demonic gaze toward him. One of them swiftly summoned a cloud of purple energy from their hands and shot a blast in his direction. Cairo jumped out of the way, leaving the explosion to destroy a few trees before disintegrating into thin air.

"Show no mercy!" one yelled, summoning another blast from his hands, but Kane landed a perfect blow to the Zealot's head before he could fire, sending him crashing to the ground in his own explosion.

Kane, Mariella, and Serenity jumped into battle, efficiently dispatching a few more Zealots, but more emerged from the woods, nearly doubling their numbers. Suddenly, Cairo, Kane, Mariella, and Serenity found themselves back-to-back, surrounded by almost two dozen Zealots.

"Guess we found the answers we need," Cairo said, chuckling. "Got any ideas up your sleeve, Kane?"

"Try to get those masks off," Kane responded shortly.

"I'll take care of that after they get this work," Cairo quipped before launching another attack.

He lunged in one direction and then darted in another with such agility that the nearest Zealot barely had time to start his incantation before Cairo drove his staff hard into the Zealot's gut, sending him crashing into another. Cairo then unleashed a vicious five-piece combination that left the hooded demon battered and sprawled on the ground.

A blast stung Cairo's back, propelling him forward. Still, he quickly rebounded by flipping off a nearby tree and connecting with another devastating kick to a Zealot, nearly knocking their mask off.

He dodged another fiery burst of purple energy and clipped another Zealot, sweeping them off their feet before landing a crushing blow to their throat.

Three more Zealots surrounded Cairo, charging for another blast, but Kane came flying in with a rod he had stolen from a fallen Zealot, connecting with a blow to the side of a head that caused one Zealot to blast the other two deep into the woods.

"Ten left," Kane said between breaths as Mariella and Serenity dispatched another three Zealots.

"Seven," Cairo countered before darting off in the direction of another Zealot. He unleashed another combination, but the Zealot was quick, dodging the critical blows and countering with a blast that hit Cairo in the chest, momentarily freezing him.

Every muscle in his body felt as if they were cramping simultaneously, forcing him to play painful defense as the Zealot continued the attack. The moment Cairo felt the effects of the magic wear off, he sidestepped the overeager Zealot and landed a massive blow to his ribs that left them reeling.

Another swipe of his staff sent the Zealot headfirst into the ground. "Six," he said to himself, kicking the unconscious Zealot into another one, driving him into a tree, "Five," he said aloud.

"Four," Serenity shouted.

"Three," Mariella countered.

"One," Kane called.

Cairo rushed in to help corner the Zealot when he heard the Zealot cackling to himself, completing an incantation that began casting projections of himself all over the place, multiplying his laughter into an annoying chorus of over fifty.

Cairo looked horrified as the Zealot and his copies completed another incantation that sent a blast at all four of them. Cairo felt his body freeze again, his muscles painfully constricting until he lost consciousness.

When he opened his eyes, everyone was gone, and he was alone in the forest by a river. Confused, he spun around several times, looking for a sign of anyone, but there was nothing. Relief washed across him as he saw his staff on the ground next to him.

As he gathered himself, he realized he was deep in the forest, as his home was now out of sight. Cairo decided to head out to find the rest of the team. Suddenly, a disturbance in the distance caught Cairo's attention. The moonlight cutting through the amber trees caught the silver demonic mask of an onlooking Zealot.

"Come on," Cairo challenged.

Emerging from the dense forest, the Zealot surged, brandishing a menacing blade. He sought any chink in Cairo's defenses, a vulnerability to exploit. However, Cairo's movements mirrored the graceful dance of the river behind him, an intricate choreography that sidestepped each probing strike. In a seamless display of agility, Cairo propelled himself backward onto his hands, limbs whirling like a helicopter's blades, striking the Zealot across the face, completely disorienting him.

A groan of agony escaped the Zealot as his sword clattered to the ground. With a fluid body contortion, Cairo suspended his legs just above the earth, executing a sweeping motion that sent the Zealot sprawling.

The thud of the Zealot's descent resonated through the air. Without contacting the ground, Cairo transitioned effortlessly into a handstand, propelling himself upward with a powerful backflip, and drove his feet squarely at the heart of the silver demonic mask worn by the Zealot. Jumping back, Cairo allowed the Zealot to rise to his feet, urging him to continue slowly.

Frustrated, the Zealot uttered a swift incantation, conjuring a pulsating orb of electric purple energy into existence. From his outstretched hands, he unleashed a barrage of crackling blasts. Undeterred, Cairo deflected the initial onslaught with his staff, an extension of his will.

Yet, the Zealot, undeterred by Cairo's defense, intensified the assault, hurling rapid-fire energy projectiles. Cairo skillfully evaded the onslaught, nimble as ever, dancing on the precipice of danger.

However, the relentless pace of the attacks left him with only enough moments to elude the imminent threat.

The climactic burst, more formidable than its predecessors, caught Cairo off-guard, the explosive impact sending him hurtling into the river. Cairo plunged deep into the depths of the river, unconscious for a moment.

Instead of succumbing to the depths, the water enveloped him in an emerald, green energy like the tender embrace of Yemaya's arms, cradling him with divine grace. He couldn't believe what was happening as he felt a new surge of life run through him. A pair of green eyes at the bottom of the river stared at him as the water guided him back to the land.

Cairo stared back at the eyes until they disappeared into the depths of the river. As he ascended out of the river, The Zealot tried to send another explosive blast in Cairo's direction, but he sidestepped and charged.

Cairo found himself within striking distance of the now-weakened Zealot. Swift as the river's current, he unleashed a thunderous uppercut, snapping the Zealot's head back and sending shockwaves through his form, causing his knees to buckle. With a mesmerizing display of skill, Cairo twirled his staff on his fingertips, delivering a forceful blow that left the Zealot unconscious while still standing.

Driving his staff into the ground, Cairo employed it as a prop for a backflip, landing a powerful kick beneath the Zealot's chin, propelling him into the air before ricocheting off a tree branch. The Zealot's purple luminescent aura faded as he lay sprawled on the ground, the unconscious victim of Cairo's skill.

Approaching cautiously, staff at the ready, Cairo prodded the fallen Zealot, flipping the body over to reveal the gleaming silver demonic mask. Disgust etched on his face, Cairo attempted to pierce the mask with his staff, but the enchanted barrier held steadfast. Frustration flared as he reached down to remove the mask with his bare hands, only to be met with a searing heat that forced a hasty retreat.

In a moment of realization, Cairo sought solace in the crystal blue tides of the river, plunging his hand into the water for relief. Cairo looked at his hands to notice the water had provided instant relief.

An idea sparked in his mind, and with renewed purpose, he seized the Zealot by the collar, dragging the unconscious body to the riverbank. Submerging the Zealot's head into the water, Cairo, undeterred by the mask's fiery resistance, tugged at it with his free hand. Miraculously, the crystal blue water surrounding Cairo's hand began to glow emerald, forming a protective barrier that allowed him to bypass the mask's fiery enchantment.

He yanked the mask free and saw that it was Maaku who dared to stand toe to toe with him. A massive surge of satisfaction crawled across Cairo's face. He tossed the mask and released Maaku, allowing the river to carry his body downstream. He stood at the bank watching the body until the tides carried him out of sight.

"Thank you, Yemaya," he said to himself, "Thank you," as the emerald-charged waters faded back to normalcy.

A sinister hiss sliced through the tranquility of the night, its malevolence sending an ominous chill down Cairo's spine. The echo of Mariella's horrified shriek followed, catapulting Cairo into action. Panic gripped his thoughts as he sprinted towards the source of the disturbance, a sense of dread gnawing at his consciousness. He summoned his scythe in the darkness, its ethereal glow cutting through the shadows.

Breaking through the dense forest, Cairo entered a moonlit clearing, where Mariella stood transfixed, her eyes locked onto the grotesque withered form of a reptilian monster sprawled before her.

Gasping for breath, Cairo found himself face to face with the surreal aftermath. "What... what happened?" he stammered, his voice betraying the uncertainty that gripped him.

"It's only skin," Mariella retorted, a wry quip cutting through the tension. "I had one of the Zealots on the ropes. They opened a portal to escape, but this thing crawled out of a purple portal."

"Are you ok?" Cairo pressed; his concern etched across his face. "Where did the portal go?"

Mariella examined the cast-off skin left by the reptilian monster, her expression thoughtful. "I'm fine, Roro; I don't know where the portal went. The Igandhi came out and snatched him up and dragged him underground with him."

A chill ran down Cairo's spine at the revelation. "Then we need to get the hell out of here and find Kane and Serenity."

Mariella nodded in agreement, and together, they plunged into the enveloping darkness.

CHAPTER 10
FOUL PLAY
KANE

Guided by the eerie moonlight, Kane navigated the foreboding forest in search of his lost group. These woods, once familiar from a lifetime of travels with Cairo, now felt different, a stillness in the air thick with tension that clung to him. The smell of smoke and pine intertwined, and Kane's run seemed endless, the same trees passing by like a haunting loop since the teleportation blast.

Amid the tense silence, the whispers had returned in an endless loop. Head swiveling, he saw nothing but nocturnal birds taking a startled flight into the night sky. The voices persisted, low and menacing, and he took off into the night as if he could outrun them, but the chants grew louder, momentarily stopping him in his tracks, before he dropped to his knees, allowing his deep breathing to help soothe the haunting sounds.

When the voices finally ceased, Kane opened his eyes and spotted a set of glowing ruby-red eyes leering at him from a nearby bush in the distance. Jumping to his feet, he approached slowly, almost in a trance. The illusion broke when he finally realized every step, he took wasn't bringing him any closer. Disappointed, he sighed, only for a hiss to permeate the air.

The chilling noise sent a shiver down Kane's spine, and Mars's ominous warning about his fateful night in the forest echoed in his head. He leaped to his feet, the hissing sound encircling him as if the reptilian presence sought to intimidate him through its calculated stalking.

Kane readied himself, settling into his defensive stance, waiting for the impending attack. The voices returned, joining the hissing in a symphony of terror, but Kane remembered his father's words. He focused his mind, still preparing for the stalking beast in the woods, and slowly, the voices began to unify until it was one solitary whisper, its message clear.

"Let go. I am with you,"

Kane felt a surge of energy, a release that cast a red aura around his entire body just as the monstrous creature leaped into the moonlight from the trees behind him. Sensing its presence, Kane flipped into the air, evading the attack, and landed a few feet away.

Before him stood the beast that had haunted his nightmares for months, nearly eye to eye with him; its green and black scaled skin reflected the moonlit sky, and its eyes filled with a look of leering death. The Ighandi cocked its head back, releasing another menacing hiss, revealing rows of razor-sharp teeth.

Kane swiftly ripped off his bracelet, transforming it into a maisha staff. With a quick motion, he summoned opposite-facing blades on each end of the staff and took his stance.

The Ighandi pounded its fists into the ground and charged wildly in Kane's direction. It swung its eagle-like talons, attempting to decapitate the prince, but Kane's instincts allowed him to dodge each one.

Frustrated, the reptilian beast lunged into the air, spinning to land a potent aerial attack. Before it could strike, Kane disconnected the rod at its center, leaving him with twin blades, and thrust one into the beast's chest.

Howling in pain, the Ighandi fell, flailing on the ground before Kane charged another attack, erupting in a burst of red energy; his blade turned crimson as he sprinted for the injured beast. With a dying effort, the Ighandi attempted a backhand that Kane slid under, thrusting his blade into the side of the reptilian.

Using his momentum, he swung his body until he could reach the handle of his other blade and forcefully yanked them both free, spewing green reptilian blood all over the forest floor. Before the reptilian's body hit the ground, Kane finished it with a quick swipe that removed its head.

The forest fell quiet, and Kane took a deep breath as he felt the energy dissipate from around him. He connected the blades and allowed the weapon to transition onto his wrist.

Looking down at the fallen beast, Kane knelt next to what had haunted his nights for nearly a year. *Was it all a warning? How in all the hell could this be happening*, he thought to himself as he finally walked away from the body.

A rustle from behind a nearby thicket interrupted his thoughts as he readied himself for another ambush, but instead of a hideous Ighandi rushing out from the foliage, Serenity revealed herself. With her gauntlets at hand, she was ready to strike until she saw Kane standing at the ready, with beads of sweat forming on his forehead.

She embraced Kane tightly, wrapping her arms around his neck. "I'm so glad you're okay!"

"Me too," Kane said softly, returning the embrace.

"I heard the hissing, and then everything went silent. I thought of one of you..." Serenity's voice trailed off into the night, refusing to say the words.

"An Ighandi found me after we got separated."

"Well, I don't see it, so you must've handled your business."

"Left me no choice. We should keep moving. We have to find Cairo and Mariella."

"How do you suppose we find them? They could be anywhere," Serenity said, staring at the endless forest surrounding them.

Kane nonchalantly shrugged his shoulders, a gesture Serenity met with a roll of her eyes. "Stop playing. Do that little thing you do."

Somewhat embarrassed, Kane shook his head, "It doesn't work like that. I'm not doing anything but following the signs."

Serenity crossed her arms, her expression filled with skepticism. "I watched you and your brother do things I can't explain for over a year. Whatever signs you need can't always pop up whenever you need them conveniently. You have to have some kind of control over it. You probably just don't know how to control it yet."

"Everyone always acts like there is a book for this stuff or something!" Kane exclaimed; frustration evident in his voice. "I'm doing my best; it's not like the Gods give me step-by-step instructions."

Serenity placed a comforting hand on Kane's shoulder, and he turned to face her soft brown eyes. "I'm not trying to put any extra pressure on you. I just see everything that you can be. I believe in you."

"Thank you," Kane replied sheepishly, but before he could utter another word, a piercing hiss tore through the stillness of the night, instantly commanding their attention. Swiftly, they dashed into the darkness, propelled by the echoing in the cry.

Upon reaching a glade in the woods, Kane spotted an Ighandi feasting on a Giant Doon in the distance. A mechanical cackle echoed through the air, jolting Kane and Serenity into a state of alertness. The Ighandi turned away from its meal, its blood-smeared face from its gore, bits of flesh still hanging from its gaping jaw. After flicking its forked tongue a few times, it turned to Kane and Serenity before conducting a chilling cry into the night sky. The Zealot shot his dark energy at the Ighandi until its eyes flashed purple.

With an ominous gesture, the Zealot reached into his pocket, extracting a handful of Xenyd. Inhaling the shimmering dust, he let its arcane properties take control, the particles weaving around him and shrouding him in an aura of pulsating purple energy.

The air crackled with an otherworldly tension as the Zealot harnessed the power of the substance; channeling an electrified purple blast, the Zealot unleashed the energy from his hands, sending it rippling in several directions.

Each charged burst hung in the air momentarily before morphing into a series of swirling portals, and from these portals emerged at least a dozen Zealots, each already pulsating with the formidable power of Xenyd, taking position by their leader.

"First, we'll end you, then your brother, and the rest of your family. After that, the Council that has hindered us for centuries will fall, ushering in a new era for Umoya!" declared the Zealot, his words resonating with a sinister determination.

Summoning more portals, the Zealot brought forth three more Ighandi onto the battlefield. The monstrous creatures aligned themselves in front of their leader, hissing and eagerly awaiting the command to attack.

Intoxicated by the surge of power, the Zealot released another robotic cackle, punctuating his triumph. Thrusting his fist into the air, he proclaimed, "Long live Shakur!"

The assembled Zealots responded fervently with the chant before their leader aimed his palm in Kane and Serenity's direction, charging for another potent blast.

Kane shut his eyes, a silent plea echoing within him, hoping that the dormant energy bestowed by the Gods would surge back to life. As the enemies closed in on him with ruthless determination, he braced for the divine empowerment that never manifested. Instead, the agonized wail of an injured Ighandi pierced the air, compelling him to open his eyes.

A pair of hatchets suddenly pierced the side of an Igandhi's head, sending the creature thrashing into another one. Emerging from the woods, Mariella and Cairo charged into the fray. The Zealots, taking notice, seized the opportunity. "Attack!" their leader screamed, unleashing a barrage of energy blasts in their direction.

Cairo and Mariella, displaying exceptional agility, effortlessly evaded the incoming attacks. They swiftly shifted into a defensive stance, skillfully dodging both Ighandi and Zealots alike. Amid the chaos, half of the Zealots redirected their focus, homing in on Kane and Serenity.

The battlefield transformed into a chaotic spectacle, with the clash of blades, the roar of Ighandi, and the crackling energy of the Zealots. Kane and Serenity found themselves in the crosshairs, the weight of the impending confrontation bearing down upon them.

Kane fought valiantly, reflecting a barrage of energy blasts with his scimitar and countering with his own strikes. However, the combined assault of Zealots and Ighandi proved overwhelming. A powerful backhand from an Ighandi sent him sprawling through the field, dazed from the impact. Sensing Kane's vulnerability, a nearby Zealot conjured a spiked wheel of purple energy and hurled it at him.

Groggy but resilient, Kane leaped into the air, narrowly avoiding the deadly projectile. During the chaos, Cairo swiftly dealt with Kane's assailant, delivering a decisive blow that incapacitated the Zealot. Kane reunited with his blade and acknowledged his brother with a quick salute before turning his attention to the remaining Ighandi.

In pursuit of the reptilian adversary, Kane faced a new danger as the Ighandi spat a wad of acidic substance. Agilely evading the attack, Kane watched in horror as the corrosive liquid struck a Zealot, transforming him into a grotesque and infected reptilian creature. Unable to escape the agony, the transformed Zealot met his end at Kane's hands.

The Ighandi, undeterred, unleashed a barrage of acidic shots, scattering the herd. Turning its attention to Kane, the creature lunged, aiming to drive its talons into Kane's chest. With swift agility, Kane dodged the assault, utilizing his twin blades to disarm the beast of its right hand.

The reptilian swiped wildly and missed, leaving it wide open for a strike with the hilt of his blade to its head and sending it reeling. At this moment, he noticed the shift in the creature's eyes from purple back to its natural yellow hue.

However, the tables turned when a Zealot ventured too close, retreating from an attack from Cairo, and was gruesomely dispatched by the Igandhi's tail. After slamming the Zealot several times, the reptilian then hurled the lifeless body toward the Zealot leader. Sensing a dire situation, the leader commanded the Ighandi to stop, attempting to regain control with a powerful spell. Before the incantation could be completed, Kane intervened, hurling his blade with all his might.

The Zealot leader, forced to evade the projectile, abandoned his spell. In retaliation, he unleashed a devastating blast that Kane attempted to block with his only remaining blade. Yet, the force was overwhelming, striking Kane square in the chest and leaving him vulnerable in the midst of the unfolding chaos.

With Kane in peril, Cairo engaged the Zealot leader, diverting his attention. Meanwhile, Kane struggled to regain his composure; his senses blurred, and his body racked with cramps, making movement nearly impossible. Using his blade as a makeshift support, he fought against the debilitating effects, managing to stagger to his feet.

Amidst the chaos, an Ighandi ran rampant, wreaking havoc and dismantling anything unfortunate enough to cross its path. Two Zealots and another Ighandi fell victim to its unbridled aggression. With Cairo occupied with the Zealot leader and Serenity and Mariella handling their own adversaries, the ferocious beast fixed its yellow gaze on the weakened Kane.

Charging toward him, the Ighandi flung its green blood in every direction with each stride. Kane, grappling with excruciating pain, tightened his grip on his blade and rolled with desperate agility, narrowly evading the wild swipes of the reptilian. Summoning all the strength he could muster, he swiftly swiped the back of the Ighandi just behind the knees, causing the creature to collapse to the ground.

In its final moments, the flailing beast attempted to unleash its acidic poison at Kane, but the agile warrior sidestepped the attack. Seizing the opportunity, Kane delivered a fatal blow, decapitating the Ighandi and putting an end to its destructive rampage.

Kane weakened and gasping for breath, took a knee to recover when he suddenly felt the onslaught of blasts from three Zealots intent on finishing him off. Their incantation wove a prison of purple energy, rendering him immobile and engulfing his body in searing pain as if a million needles pierced his every fiber. Agony compelled him to scream, but amidst the chaos of the battlefield, his cries went unheard.

The Zealots reveled in their sadistic triumph, mocking Kane's helplessness. Unable to resist, he closed his eyes, summoning the last reserves of his strength in a desperate attempt to break free. At that moment, a sudden sensation enveloped him, a profound numbness that replaced the excruciating pain.

As Kane surrendered to the stillness, a profound energy within him began churning. With his eyes closed, he yielded to the internal force. Suddenly, a burst of red energy erupted from him, sending all three Zealots hurtling into the air. The explosive display caught the attention of the entire battlefield as Kane's aura ignited in a crimson glow.

Every fiber of his being surged with the energy of the Gods, granting him newfound abilities; he moved with speed previously unknown to him, a crimson blur on the battlefield, turning the tide of the confrontation with a power that transcended Umoyan limitations. The once-vulnerable Kane had become a force to be reckoned with, and the battle atmosphere shifted with the undeniable presence of divine energy.

In a whirlwind of motion, Kane swiftly disposed of the three Zealots that had sought to bind him in their purple energy trap. His relentless attacks left each Zealot maimed and bleeding on the battlefield. Meanwhile, Serenity and Mariella grappled with the remaining six Zealots, and Cairo engaged in a fierce battle with the Zealot leader and the Ighandi under his command.

Kane charged forward, reclaiming his missing blade with a fluid grace. Reconnecting his scimitar at its center, he focused his newfound speed on the unruly Ighandi. The creature, lacking the discipline to control its attacks, succumbed to Kane's agile onslaught. Seizing an opening, Kane delivered a devastating blow to the beast's head, breaking the spell that had ensnared it.

With the Ighandi now free, Kane observed an opportunity to disrupt the Zealot leader's attack on Cairo. An uppercut launched the leader into the air, and Cairo, seizing the moment, delivered a decisive blow to the leader's mask with his staff. The impact sent the leader hurtling toward the now-liberated Ighandi.

Unaware of the creature's newfound freedom, the Zealot leader turned his back on it, commanding an attack. Instead, the Ighandi hissed and lashed out, leaving a deep gash across the leader's back. Panic set in as the leader attempted to cast another spell, but the agile Ighandi evaded it and retaliated with an acidic shot that connected with the leader's mask.

With the Ighandi still fixated on their leader, Cairo swiftly thrusted his scythe through the reptilian's chest from behind. A lethal twist sent the creature plummeting into the realm of lifeless echoes. However, horror unveiled itself when the Zealot leader, writhing in pain, tore off his mask, revealing none other than Donovan, the Zion prince.

In agony, Donovan's screams harmonized with the rapid spread of the infection, a malevolent force devouring hands and arms alike. The battlefield bore witness, a haunting silence lingering in its aftermath. Amidst the solemnity, Kane took a deep breath, allowing the crimson energy to dissipate and his mind to replay the ominous vision from Ganyah's party.

The Gods were trying to tell me all along, he thought to himself.

With a decisive swipe, Kane severed the prince's head.

"Well, well, well," a voice materialized from behind. Without turning, Kane recognized it as his aunt Shareeva's. "What do we have here?"

Shareeva, accompanied by Mara, emerged from the forest, their arrival shrouded in mystery. "Wha...what happened here?" Mara asked as they drew nearer. Kane, Cairo, Serenity, and Mariella remained vigilant, weapons poised, uncertain if the danger had truly subsided.

"What in the hell are you doing here?" Kane barked, his voice carrying the authority of a manticore's roar. "Don't you dare take another step closer!"

"Donovan?" Mara whimpered, her voice fragile. "Oh no, not my sweet Donovan!"

She sprinted toward her son's lifeless form, his head severed, collapsing to her knees. Tears welled in her eyes like a storm gathering momentum. "How could you! How could you do this to my son?"

"Your son was a Zealot, and he got what he deserved!" Cairo threatened a dark edge to his words. "I know all of you are involved in this. It's over for all of you; I promise you that."

"My son... Shareeva!" Mara screamed, her voice resonating across the grasslands. "My son is dead!"

"Mara, listen to me! We will work all of this out!" Shareeva spat, the words bearing a stern weight, as Mara slowly rose.

"My husband and son were ripped away from me! No! This is not how this is supposed to unfold! They should be with me right now!"

"We must consider how this affects the realm. We have to handle this the proper way!"

"Oh, I plan to handle it. A family for a family!"

"Mara, calm down," Shareeva urged, but Mara paid no heed.

"What have you lost, huh?" Mara screamed, taking a step closer to Shareeva, "I lost everything tonight while you sit there, looking down on me? How can you sit there and act like you—"

Before Mara could finish her sentence, Shareeva pointed her delicate, long finger at Mara's forehead. A purple dart of energy, swift as an arrow, struck Mara right between the eyes, snuffing out her life instantly. She fell dead beside her decapitated son.

Kane, Cairo, Serenity, and Mariella leaped back-to-back, scanning frantically to identify the source of the lethal shot. Shareeva stood calm amidst the chaos.

"Shareeva, no!" Kane stammered, his disbelief echoing through the air. "We could have brought her before the council!"

"And you would have been standing trial right next to her! The blood of the prince is on all your hands!"

"He was planning on killing our father!" Cairo shouted, his anger a wildfire. "Every one of those Zealots got off easier than they deserved. They should have suffered a slower death!"

"And you right along with them!" Serenity added her condemnation.

"So, I do nothing but try to help, and you still call for my life? Make it make sense!" Shareeva scoffed. "I'm the one who has been trying to maintain peace between the council and Zion!"

"You're lying!" Mariella screamed.

"Your mother sought my aid in the first place!" Shareeva retorted. "But, as usual, all of you think you know everything! It was me who attempted to keep the peace, me who alerted the council about the impending attacks."

"Why should we believe a word you say? My brother warned me not to trust you because you were dabbling in dark magic again!"

"And how did you know about the attacks if you weren't involved?" Serenity questioned; suspicion etched on her face.

"The same way I knew you were out here in the first place! I've been tracking you," Shareeva replied calmly.

Shareeva turned to the forest, her voice cutting through the tension. "I just wish we would've gotten here sooner. You can come out now, Keiko."

From the woods emerged an almond-colored woman with locks cascading down her back, clad in a camouflage outfit that seamlessly blended with the surroundings. She expertly dismantled her rifle, casting a confident gaze upon each of them.

"That's one of the girls from the bar," Mariella whispered.

"I thought I recognized her face," Serenity added.

"Keiko here has been helping uncover the truth about the

Zealots. I'm pretty sure behind each of these masks is a face that you recognize. They were plotting to overthrow the entire council."

"And you expect us to believe that you had no idea Donovan was the leader of the cult?" Cairo scoffed. "I'm not buying it!"

"Luckily, I'm not selling you anything, and no, I didn't know Donovan was involved. I just knew that there was a cult using ancient dark magic, and they were behind the kidnappings. I found out they were feeding innocent Umoyans in the Ighandi they were breeding, and Ms. Mekari lost her life trying to reveal that secret."

"Why not go to Mom?" Kane inquired reluctantly.

"I just told you, when I found out, I warned the entire council."

"What do we do here, Kane?" Cairo asked. "I say we kill this witch, rid the whole realm of all this dark magic stuff once and for all!"

"Cairo, don't be foolish; why kill me? Now listen, the way I see it, we can either march to your mother, tell her everything we just witnessed, and deal with whatever comes with that. Or Keiko and I can take care of all this mess for you, and you can still go on your little death quest, and the realm will know the truth it needs."

"And what truth is that?" Kane asked.

"That Mara and her family secretly plotted against the council, and they fell victim to their own devious schemes, trying to control beasts that should have never been brought back from the pit of the lowest hell."

In Kane's heart, he wanted to reject Shareeva's plan, but everything in his body knew it was the best option. The truth would ruin the realm, shattering the fabric that held it together. With the problems of Zion gone and the Zealots dispatched, the realm would be in a position to heal right before they would embark on the quest.

"Let's go, y'all," Kane finally uttered.

"Are you serious?" Cairo asked, finally relaxing his weapon in surprise. "You really are going to follow her plan?"

"What choice do we have? Look at all of this! At least with this, everything dies with them, and we control the narrative. We have a shot to create real peace."

"I agree," Serenity admitted reluctantly after weighing Kane's thoughts briefly.

"Me too," Mariella added.

"Fine, whatever," said Cairo in disbelief.

"Keiko, get the girls and take care of this while I take these kids back to the city."

With a slight nod, Keiko began organizing the bodies for transport as Shareeva led the way back to the city. Kane watched slowly, ensuring he remained a few feet behind, hoping for any subtle sign from the Gods that they were making the right decision.

When they finally made it, with the city on the horizon, Kane slowed to a halt, watching as ash fell from the skies. The whispers returned, and Kane instinctively focused on clearly deciphering the message.

"It has begun," the voice repeated, until finally, in the blink of an eye, the entire city erupted into flames, engulfed in chaos. Cairo, Serenity, and Mariella had suddenly disappeared, leaving only Shareeva heading into the burning village, covered in a purple aura.

Noticing Kane had stopped, Cairo secretly got Serenity's and Mariella's attention and turned towards his brother, nudging him until the vision finally broke.

"You okay, bro?" he asked.

Kane shook his head, eyeing Shareeva as if he had seen a ghost. "It's not over," he said, looking back at the seemingly peaceful city. "It's not over."

THE END

Made in the USA
Columbia, SC
26 May 2024

35742432R00076